The Sea Change

The Sea Change

A True Tale of High Adventure

John S. Bohne
9/11/01

by

John S. Bohne

ISBN: 0-75960-235-2

This book is printed on acid free paper.

1stBooks. –rev. 2/12/01

THE SEA CHANGE

The Flying Kate

"But O, the ship,
the immortal ship!

O ship aboard
the ship!

Ship of the body,
ship of the soul,

Voyaging, voyaging,
voyaging."

-Walt Whitman

The Flying Kate
Wilmington Harbor, CA

Captain Lamont's native love, Tiee.

*** *** *** ***

Found Shangri-La—He's Going Back

* * * * * * * * * * * *

Skipper, 38, Building Ship Here; Hunts Adventurers for Voyage to S. Pacific

Capt. Allan Lamont (right) and his first mate, Robert Wetherley, inspect Yankee Clipper picture mounted in reception room of SUN-TIMES news department. (SUN-TIMES Photo)

Skipper, 38, Building Ship Here; Hunts Adventurers for Voyage to S. Pacific

Skipper Builds Ship for Return to Shangri-La

Capt. Allan Lamont (right) and his first mate, Robert Wetherley, Inspect Yankee Clipper picture mounted in reception room of SUN-TIMES news department.
(CHICAGO SUN TIMES Photo)

Lenora Lost:::

There were moments of stark tragedy, too. He cited the case of his lovely Eurasian wife, half-Chinese, half-white.

Devoted, Resourceful

She was devoted, resourceful and a sharp hand at bargaining. Then came the day she told hem she was leaving, and before he could ask why, she said:

"I have leprosy."

He saw her slip over the side of the ship in a heavy..sea and vanish.

SON OF SINGER

Lamont is the son of a Russian opera singer and Corsican French soldier.

Building a Ship

But, Lamont declared, he's through now with landlubbering. He is trying to locate his old crew and a few more adventurous souls who would like to return with him to the island.

And to that end, he and his first mate, Robert Wetherley, 35, are building a 44-foot seagoing two-master—right here at Belmont and the Chicago River.

"I don't think I'm trying to run away from the world," Lamont said thoughtfully. "People should stay to reshape the world they live in. I'm going to help add to that world by going back to Shangri-La.

SON OF SINGER

Lamont is the son of a Russian opera singer and Corsican soldier.

There were moments of stark tragedy, too. He cited the case of his lovely Eurasian wife, half-Chinese, half-white.

DEVOTED, RESOURCEFUL

She was devoted, resourceful and a sharp hand at bargaining. Then came the day she told him she was leaving, and before he could ask why, she said:

"I have leprosy."

He saw her slip over the side of the boat in a heavy [illegible]

BUILDING A SHIP

But, Lamont declared, he's through now with landlubbering. He is trying to locate his old crew and a few more adventurous souls who would like to return with him to the island.

And to that end, he and his first mate, Robert Wetherley, 35, are building a 44-foot seagoing two-master—right here at Belmont and the Chicago River.

"I don't think I'm trying to run away from the world," Lamont said thoughtfully. "People should stay to reshape the world they live in. I'm going to help add to that world by going back to Shangri-La."

SACRAMENTO 2 - 9294 — 9257

Midwest Hotel - Capone

Showtime Lounge

CONTINUOUS ENTERTAINMENT — OPEN LATE

3814 W. MADISON ST. 388 CHICAGO

8/4/50

Rec'd of John [illegible]

$500.00 Five Hundred Dollars

Matthew Capone

Cosco Enterprises

Figure 1

Author on Dock - Ship background

Figure 2

Author on stern

Figure 3

Steve Stover (deceased)

Figure 4

Steve

Figure 5

Steve

Figure 6

Wilmington Harbor - San Pedro waterfront - California

Figure 7

Mexico & 1950 Studabaker

Figure 8

C.I.A. & Steve

PROLOUGE

The sun comes up
The sun goes down

The sun comes up
The sun goes down

The sun comes up
The sun goes down

Young spirits are
Pressed to the ground.

The raging storm of the Great War was over, and we were left in the doldrums. The Goddess Ennui had our small town by the throat. We were being driven to distraction. Nothing was happening every minute.

She created 14 taverns in Oak Lawn, Illinois…and drove the good citizens to drink. Her rule is cruel. We could not abide dulling drink. We formed up the Hometown Four against the Bore. Climbed the water tower and painted an "S" before OAK LAWN up there. (You know how the young are)

Ah Yes, the Hometown Four? Myself, reporter of the Oak Lawn Independent, Guadalcanal Marine, N.U. student, poet and writer. Most important: Capt Allan Lamont's secret weapon. (which he always called me) He knew that I would write the story of a great sea Captain. A promise. That is the reason this book is being done. Do not need money, don't want fame. Refuse to play the game. But other promises have held the story in Limbo long enough….it can finally be told. My function. Fabulous Captain. Strange ship, Odd crew, Write it! Has become a ghost ship. "The Flying Kate" is blown. Ted Winkle—flaky, but brilliant in mind. Likeable. Steve Stover—a young bull. Handsome. Ready for anything. Mean. Willy Woeman—a screw loose somewhere. A pyro. (as reporter got a strong suspicion from his happy presence at burning barns and sheds)

Near our town the bleached bones of a monster lay upon the green countryside—the abandoned Syndicate Race-Track. It had taken the money of the town in those innocent $2.00 bets, and was now a galore eye-sore. We voted to torch it. Make a Nero night the town folk could talk about for a long time.

We put Willy at the heart of it with a 5 gal can of gasoline. He loved fire so much he would have set it directly...and perhaps happy to go to Hell. But we made a runner of gas-soaked old clothes to save his skinny behind.

Dark night. A fiery cloud of flame leaped up above the bleachers! We set the ends of the board skeleton burning fierce. The conflagration turned the sky red for miles around! The Nero night! Willy had wet his pants. Had to get him out of there...as we could hear sirens in the distance. We had given him his greatest night. Yet, but then, the Goddess came creeping back in to town worse then ever...time was on her side.

THEN IT HAPPENED!!!! Ted came running with the story of a Captain Allan Lamont who was looking for a crew to man his ship out to the South Seas. It was in the Chicago SUN-TIMES. They had a photo of him pointing to a sailing ship in the reception room.

I was elected to go see the Captain at once.

Dedicated to all lonely people who lead lives of quiet desperation devoid of adventure

The Sea Wind Blows

Chapter 1

The Grebe boatyard on the Chicago River was a Boomer from The Great War. Yachts and PT boats were worked on from a series of sheds and out-buildings. A sleek white yacht was being constructed on the ways. The rich had a thing going here.

The Captain's location was in a dingy corner, and on a smelly backwater. An echo of the Bubbly Creek reputation of the River. A ramshackle building was falling into ruin. Untoward odors pervaded the place. Rotting wood, unmoving murky waters in a dismal atmosphere. It was below the bottom of the barrel in the nautical world. Hardly the location for a sea-going ship.

Suspicions started to nag me.

There was a huge EATERY sign. In the doorway stood a big woman.

"I'm Marie Shrimp. Looking for the Captain?" she asked, "Come in for a cup of coffee on me, and we will talk."

Following behind the buxom woman there came the feeling of a madam of a house of repute. She was the type. My wonderings increased. A large diamond sparkled on her finger. The Captain did not get that as yet…a good sign.

She was reading me. "That diamond is in reserve if he ever needs it."

She was eager to talk about herself and the Captain. She was in love with him! A really good sign…love is usually positive.

Where was he? And what was the ship like?

I drank some coffee and waited.

She sat down heavily. Smiled at my silence.

"Came over from Italy to Corsica. He lived on the island. Father was a soldier…actually a French General, and mother an Opera singer from Russia. Royalty. They lived in a stone house up on a hill near town. Loved Lamont right from when I saw him. A really handsome and exciting man!"

"Italy?" I inquired, "What about your name?"

"Had a long Italian name. The Captain said to shorten it and have mercy on mankind. We were down by the docks where I ran an eating place for sea folk. He looked around and saw those little buggers of the sea. Shrimp! People will remember you. It has worked wonders for me. He has the confidence to command any situation. He is a wonder!

Her eyes were as bright as the diamond on her finger.

"Is he a Captain?" I dared ask.

"Not a paper one like so many who foul up at sea...do you know how many docks have been knocked to hell by ships? He is a natural. He can do whatever he thinks to do...and does it extremely well...Trust Him!"

"That photo in the Sun-Times? His mate looks a bit wily."

"Watch out for that skinny weasel. He is as slippery as a lemon seed. He does free the Captain of small tasks in life. Hey, look, the Captain is a Master of right motion whether on the sea or the Ocean of Life...in return he helps his side-kick steer a straight course. He does not think small thoughts much, and he lives up above money. He needs a helper."

She looked hard at me.

"Captain Allan Lamont is a direct descendent of Napoleon!"

"Whoa, whoa!" I exclaimed.

She threw back her head and laughed, the way a big woman of the world will do.

"Let me tell you something," she said, "Ever been to the Newberry Library? The scholars there have a high respect for the Captain. They know who he is. There is a dark place in his life—the lost Lenora. A deep sorrow. He had a sailing ship, the Ramona. Was on the way to Tahiti. She was a perfect beauty, but found spots of leprosy on herself. Loved him so much, she just went off the stern in a heavy sea. It was beyond his command. She sank away in the sea. She was half white and half Chinese. He has a native girl, Tiee, in Tahiti...but no one can replace Lenora. The light of his life is gone."

"That is sad." I agreed.

"He is down there working on a boat." she directed.

His back was to me. He was stuffing pitch into cracks of a life-boat, from a ship long gone. His gray coveralls had splotches of tar on them. He did not appear to be in good circumstances. No ship here.

He turned toward me…and I was looking at a Clark Gable. Amazingly handsome man with dark eyes and a Mona Lisa like smile, that you knew was perpetual. His bearing said CAPTAIN. His eyes agreed with Marie's diamond.

"It was a great story in the Times. Now we need to make it come true for us. Like to work on any boat at all for now."

"Yes, but…"

"Fools can ask questions that wise men can't answer, and you are not a fool."

He walked away toward the EATERY. Spun on his heel and came back.

"I smell the sea wind blowing. We are going. I will get us a ship. Go and gather a crew. Marie will provide a phone no. for contact in two weeks.

"Yes, my Captain." I heard myself reply. Rapport right off. I believed in him fully.

Chapter 2

Back in town before the Four all I had was a phone number.

Steve was getting mad. He wanted to see a ship as in the news story. "Where the hell is it?" he yelled at me, "A life-boat will not do."

"Don't press him," Ted advised. "Let him handle it."

"This Captain will get you to sea." I insisted. "Just give him some time!"

"What do we have to do now?" Willy wanted to know.

"Wait and see what happens" I said.

A phone call produced an address. The Captain wanted to see me near the Loop in Chicago.

The neighborhood was low class. He was staying with an Italian widow whose husband had been killed on a motor schooter by a truck. The spaghetti dinners were excellent. He was thinking.

The room was dingy. No improvement over the boatyard at all. The glass mirror over the dresser had a bunch of rubber monkeys on it.

He gave them a hit. They wiggled around, and kept on going for a time.

"Thought projection," he explained, "Sort out the complexities of the complex—and make them simple for action."

"God bless you, Captain." I replied, "We have four for a crew, and now it's money, of course?"

"A necessary tool to work the machine of the world. It serves as oil too."

"$500 each," I offered.

"Good enough. I can make up for low funds." he said.

His appearance had changed. It was amazing! He had on a natty waist-coat of a Captain's cut. But there was a black Homburg hat instead of the captain hat. He handled a gold-headed cane as if it were a royal scepter. No mere Captain. Kingly! It made you think he had a country somewhere. There was no indication of a deep sorrow. He was in command of the world. Debonair!

"I want you to accompany me in social circles as we seek a ship," he stated. "You are my secret weapon." he said, without an explanation. "The playboys have ships, rather boats. The cargo-haulers have ships. Ocean liners are out too. We need a special ship. We must look for it. Find someone who has it. Only then will it get easy."

His smile increased.

"I am a conner, not a con man. The way a Captain is with a ship. I never take anything unless it is offered. We must work our way thru the waters of the Dark Ocean." he revealed.

Finally it dawned on me that his secret weapon in life is a writer. Well, I would be it for him. No writer ever had better dream come true than this. Fabulous!

I made him a promise to write his story for the world.

The widow had a young daughter, lovely enough to be tempting to men. She was fascinated by Lamont. He acted as a father for her. A good man.

I left the Captain to work his monkeys, and waited to hear from him by phone.

Ted was caught in the dream. He was highly impressed with what he heard from me...and with the way I was reacting. He was eager to move. He had access to money. He sent the Captain $2000.

There was an immediate response. The Captain wanted to meet his crew...look them over. He informed me they would be some part of a plan he was thinking out for some action.

"Good!" I replied. "Action is what they want. Ted is starting to dream about it. Steve is like a bull ready to charge. And Willy and I are eagerly waiting for it. We are ready. We need to get moving soon!"

"Get them to wear khaki clothes, tropical grade. I want them to start looking like a crew. Start to think Tropics. A military aspect will work well too."

Bob, the Captain's useful shadow, was kept behind in the background base. His furtive eyes and snively way would be a drag up front now. He was helping the widow wash clothes. Lamont had noted "the first mate" had struck a sour note at the Sun-Times office. No command confidence there.

"I thank you for using your vehicle to get us around," he said, "We must go places to get action going." I was happy with it. It gave me conversations in the car with him alone. It was already an adventure!

We went for a brief sojourn on the Gold coast of Chicago---right to the Drake Hotel! The target was Wrigley, the Gum King! Lamont engaged him in conversation in the restaurant. He was caught up in the dream. But then the Captain dropped him cold.

There were nights in the Clubs on Rush St. and Division St....seekings among men at pleasure. Amazing talks! But who has a real ship in his pocket? Everyone loved the Captain's dream. Word about the Captain started to get around like wildfire.

The world of strippers too. They flocked around Captain Lamont like flies around a candy cane. God, how they went for him! Instead of him filling their palms, they would give him money...helping the dream. Strippers! Rare! Very rare! Amazing to see it happen! At Harry's New Yorker, Laura, in admiration, informed him, "You are the talk of the town. The girls are waiting to meet you at all the Clubs. Go to it!"

"Can't spend too much time going around," he replied, "You know I'm pursuing a ship to go to sea. Bless the girls, but the sea has my love."

He was speaking of Leona.

But he would use women as support bases, and get operating expenses from them. ???I dared ask him about this—and he replied directly—"They love it, and me too...because I do love them. Some adventure comes into their mundane lives. I touch their lives like an artist painting a picture. It is a joy to do it."

"What do you do to them?" I dared to ask.

"I take them up to where most women never get to go---the Seventh heaven!" he said gently.

Marie Shrimp was right about him.

Finally the Arabian nights ended in no ship. The crew was unhappy, and prospects were dim. A ship is not easy to get—in fact, extremely difficult to acquire—even for a genius. A dismal end to it seemed imminent.

But the Captain's voice over the phone was in high spirits: "Meet me at the Midwest Hotel this afternoon," he said. "Bring the crew."

Walking down State Street he had been a spectacle. Going down the street in this drab neighborhood with his crew, he was a shining star. People thought they were seeing a celebrity, even a king. They made way for him.

The Midwest Hotel is not an imposing structure. What were we doing here?

We headed for the Showtime Lounge inside.

The Captain stepped in the door and ordered—"Make way for my crew!" The noisy drinkers did. We marched through the crowd to a table by the stage...which was made available quickly. But the Captain did not sit down. "To the bar," he ordered his crew. His cane was at work, and the black Homburg took a jaunty angle on his head. People stared in amazement. Kingly!

He came up to a rather rotund man at the bar. Drinkers slid down to open up seats. Lamont threw $2000 cash on the bar and said: "Give everyone in the house a drink!"

The bar was not packed. Fortunately, I thought.

He sat down next to Matt Capone, and engaged him in lively conversation. Capone was impressed. "My ship is docked up the Hudson River," he told Capone.

"Come up to my room, and I'll put on a clean shirt and tie, and we will go to New York now." Capone said to Lamont.

"Excellent," the Captain agreed, "One of my crew will come along."

Upstairs there was a picture on the wall of Mama, and her brood of violent sons...all with staring eyes and round faces with the look of dead fish. Her name was Theresa, husband Gabriel. Neapolitans from Italy. The Capone Family! Al had his expensive white felt hat on and stood out...white spats too.

"Al is dead three years now and buried in Mt. Carmel Cemetery." Matt lamented. "He was King of Chicago and had it all...and I had it all too. No more now. Left me in bad circumstances. The cops harass me down on the street. Have made me a police character. Trying to drive me out of Chicago. I'm not a bad guy. It's the name. Why don't they bother those maroons down there instead of me?"

Matt's paranoia repeated itself: "I get so mad about those maroons down on the street," Matt said sadly, "My name is mud now, but they are

O.K. for Chicago to have around. They got me down the lowest of all. That's not fair!"

"You have the name hanging around your neck like the albatross of 'The Ancient Mariner' and must go around like 'The Wandering Jew,'" Lamont reflected.

"I never had anything to do with those guys," Matt protested, "Who the hell are they?"

"The Ancient Mariner is a psychology poem, and the Jew who struck Jesus when he was dying had a curse put on him to wander restless the world forever." Lamont answered him gently. "Just a poem and a legend."

"The hell with that stuff!" Matt said.

"People are prejudiced," the Captain said, "If you come with me you will be able to stand on your own two feet."

Matt beamed at him.

"I was the kid brother. Mama said to Al, 'You keep him out of the rackets. He is my baby.' Al was afraid to argue with her. She hit him hard on the back with her rolling pin once, good and hard! He could not hit back. You hit your mother in the Italian world, and your name is mud. No one will work with you. She is the only person Al was afraid of in life," Matt said proudly.

"That's very revealing, Matt," the Captain commented.

"You know about Ralph? He ran a big brewery to make the bootleg stuff. They called him 'Bottles.' He did a damn good business too." Matt said proudly. "Al was just a business man too."

"You present a good case that men should not live for money." The Captain concluded.

Chapter 3

There was a speedboat waiting at the dock on the Hudson in N.Y.C. Despite his bum status, Capone had ordered it. He had told the Captain that people owed Al favors in New York. Going up the river, Lamont saw a large ship docked up…and no activity.

"There she is." Lamont said.

We went aboard, and down into the hold. The Captain took out his pocket-knife, went over to a beam, and removed a bit of wood. "Dry rot!" he exclaimed, "Standing too long. Not seaworthy anymore."

"Hell," Capone reacted, "Let's go to The Circle Club this afternoon. There's a guy there who had a ship in Alaska recently. Abe Danches. He's a Hollywood producer. Made some sort of a B movie out there. We might get it if it is still around."

The Circle Club was in the plush quarters of a canyon building, high up above the streets. Exclusive to members. Matt got us in. (the old days were still working…fear, money, power, whatever)

Seated around at a table were men of various influences who could plot, plan, deal, and function in their own little world of interest…a back-scratchers organization---The Circle Club! They were talking over current affairs. They looked askance at Capone. Abe Danches was among them. He regarded the Captain with interest.

Matt was direct. "Do you still have that ship from Alaska?" he inquired of Danches.

"Why, Yes. 'The Flying Kate' is anchored in Wilmington Harbor out in California. What about it?"

"We need it." Matt informed him.

"Well, it's just sitting there. Have no need for it. Would require some work. What deal can we make?"

"How about running some contraband stuff for good profits?" Matt offered.

"Damn, no deal! Keep my name out of it! You can take the damn ship!" Abe exclaimed much upset.

"O.K., Captain Lamont, you got a ship!" Matt said proudly. "What was that movie, Abe?"

"The Son of Vengeance" Abe said, "The ship is built of heavy planks not painted, has a powerful diesel motor, one screw, two masts, and a high bow. Been there for awhile now. Not neat, but damn strong. Will need work. It's not called 'The Flying Kate' for nothing—only 104 ft long with that motor it will move. It's a very fast ship! Might even be able to outrun the people you will have after you! Good Luck!"

Captain Lamont had scored. The dream! The ship! I could see he was eager to board her. He was ready to turn Captain of the Sea. Steve would be happy now, Ted would be justified, Willy would want to inspect the galley stove, and for myself the old Marine Corps spirit was awakened to the sea. Adventure was calling us!

Back in town each of us got the $500 up. The town lawyer, our friend, drew up a contract of Ansco Enterprises for all to sign. No charge to us. Everyone wants a part of an adventure. He was worried about Capone being in on it. After all, he had seen bodies dumped in cornfields around our town. The Capone Era was real to Oak Lawn. All signed, Capone did not. He only signed a receipt for me for $500…as the Captain had informed me Capone was broke and needed some operating funds. (he did get the ship for us) (actually, he indulged himself right off by buying an expensive silk shirt and tie…as he was trying to live in the past when…"His brother Al was King and he Matt had it all too!") His lament as kid brother was rather moronic.

But finally he said to the Captain: "I need to get out of Chicago before they have me with Al in the marble orchard. I'm going with you."

"Good," Lamont agreed, "The sea can do wonders for you. You need a change in your life. John has a 1950 Studebaker. It's that Starlight Coupe model, with the wrap-around windows in the back…you can watch the stars on the way to the ship. He will take you out to the West Coast. Phone him your pick-up point."

The sea wind was blowing strong, and we all needed to get out to the ship and work on it. Everyone started across the vast U.S. I was left with Capone. In my estimation he was a moron. I knew it would be a dicey go in my vehicle.

At the street corner near the Midwest Hotel, there was Matt...and he had a tall red-headed fellow named Harry with him. He had a gun under his armpit. Harry was to go along for the ride, "So nothing would happen to us." Great! He just piled into the back seat. Perhaps Capone thought I was going to kidnap him. But he was not worth anything anymore. Nor did I have any such inclinations. What would I do with a gangster moron?

In travels across the U.S. I carry a Western style revolver, Double Nine, ivory handle, 9 shot cylinder, 22 long rifle cartridges. No automatic to jam up. It's a marksman's pistol. You aim each bullet to the target. No need for heavy stuff and a lot of fire power. And it's a show piece. A previous pistol had been worn out to an open bore by firing of over 100,000 shots. A 22 pistol is like my right hand. Had killed a duck on the water at a quarter of a mile, and shot a sparrow out of a tree at 75 yds. Harry did not know it but he was at a stand-off. It's nice to have this kind of insurance.

Matt was not a good traveler. He started bitching right off. Strain was showing on a too fat guy out of shape. It was going to be a hard go.

Talking about the past, he took the wheel outside of Chicago. "Learned some tricks in the bootleg days," he informed us. He jerked the wheel about while going around a curve at high speed. "Get around much faster by making the front wheels jump." he explained. He almost hit a car head on.

At the next stop I got Red aside. "Red," I said, "Do you want to live?"

"Hell, Yes!"

"Let's get Matt in the back seat then." I suggested.

"Good idea," he agreed.

Matt went into a huff in the back seat. He cursed at us. "Why you punks, guys were killed for less than this in the old days. You insult me!"

"Yes Matt," I foolishly revealed to him, "I saw the photo of you bandaged up in a hospital bed after going thru that poor farmer's house with that big black Packard! You did the curve nice that time. Went right past that sucker's bed, and almost killed his kids too. Ruined the guy's house. Bet you never paid him either."

"You lousy punk," he retorted, "How did you know that?"

"Herald-American morgue. Press people work together. Sort of a brotherhood, just like your Syndicate. There was a manila envelope on every year of your life."

"That was just an accident. I was coming home from a wild party outside of the city...had too much to drink...went to sleep. That's Legit! Al just laughed about it. Why when he was the King..."

"Stop living in the past, Matt. It's over!" I told him.

Matt got morose in the back seat. He pouted like a little kid. He was mumbling, "Punks, punks, just punks."

"One thing yet, Matt," I added, "You killed a guy in an alley behind a Club."

"Just a rat, just a rat. He owed me a gambling debt. Refused to pay me. No one was in the alley. I shot him with Al's personal gun. Al liked it a lot." Matt bragged.

"The gun or what you did?"

"Knocking the guy off is what made Al laugh. He told me I was a chip off the old block. It was a matter of money and needed taking care of."

We headed out of Chicago on old 66, and then took 40, finally cutting up to Las Vegas. Near summer season. It was a hot trip. On reaching the desert, I took out the pistol for some practice. Red was driving, and he watched me with much interest. Going along about 60 m.p.h., I lined up on a jack-rabbit running alongside nearby. The third shot rolled him over.

"God, I would not want to come up against you." Red said.

Actually I was doing it for Matt. His eyes grew wide open. He was getting it. "Matt, if you ever send someone after me...he get's it...and then you get it!" I said firmly. He bought my bluff. Those who do killing think all men are killers at heart. But I felt bad about the rabbit. (the Guadalcanal experience had turned me against violence, and the death of all living things) Now I agree with The White Robe Brothers—no killing. Even more have become a Christian yogi in spiritual thought.

The days rolled along. Red had never seen the desert or the mountains. He was enjoying it immensely. He was willing to fill the tank a few times to help out. Not a bad guy. Matt reacted to sights with a mild indifference—his world was Chicago. He sewed up his purse, and had another for contributions from whoever wherever.

The desert was extremely hot! Finally making the turn toward Las Vegas, we drove toward the great orange orb of the setting sun on the horizon. Its brilliance blinded us. Our eyes were like marbles in our head. Matt was hiding under a towel. But he came alive. "Go to the Charley White Club," he directed.

Down the Strip, and inside, he talked with someone who appeared to be a manager. He would not let me near to hear the conversation. (the envelopes were haunting me now) But I marked what I could in a small red book. At least stop points. We did a few.

There was Jimmy Durante. He became apprehensive about Matt. Knew him. Matt went up to him, and told him about the ship.

"The boys all put in 5 C's. We need travel money bad."

Durante reached in his pocket, took out the hundred dollar bills, gave them to Matt. He believed in travel—travel away from him. And so did some others around the Clubs, not even stars...giving varying amounts to Matt. We did not know just what was going on for this to happen. Staying on the safe side of him? Not knowing he was a bum in Chicago? Was being a bum possible in the Syndicate? We had no way to know anything for sure, nor did others too. Matt had insisted we go thru Las Vegas. It was a money trip for him. It would seem he considered a little shakedown was good for the soul...well, for the pocket anyway. Once the second purse was full, we could travel on to the ship. Good ole Matt. But us bees were not going to get any of the honey. The Capones are not built that way. (but Al was generous—for business purposes—and to stay alive)

But away! To the ship and a new day! Fresh out of Northwestern University and to an adventure! (actually, the adventure) The Navy song instead of The Marine Hymn. "Say goodbye to college joys, we sail at the break of day...away, away, away." I was in good spirits! Our Captain must already be at the ship?

California, the promised land, looked good to us. It contained our ship. Our spirits soared high when we saw it out in Wilmington Harbor. It stood out singular amid the many craft anchored around in the Harbor.

"The Flying Kate" was really one-of-kind! Strange like a tramp steamer in a mystery.

Matt went into a motel by the dock. He registered as Randolph Hunter. (as a writer, I thought of putting him in charge of names for characters) This was to be his abode, while we were to live aboard the ship.

But where was the Captain? No sign of him.

I put my baggage and supplies on the dock. Rang the bell for the water taxi. It came after a bit of time, and took me out to the ship. As the small boat neared "The Flying Kate" the ship became more impressive right along. It was different, and strange. A sturdy ship.

Steve, Ted, and Willy were living aboard. They had taken up residence in the hull with glee. They greeted me with happy shouts. They said the Captain had organized half of the San Pedro waterfront already. What?

The Captain was in his glory! Girls! Men getting interested in his dream. He had it all going—and it was going all right. Soon there would be operating funds. Talk about him winged its way around the waterfront. He was becoming the toast of the sea-farers. Our Captain! The South Sea island dream rests in the hearts of all men. He had been aboard the ship and told the crew he had fallen in love with it—it was it! He said it was a special ship!

"No pillows or sheets for the bunks," Willy complained.

Steve had done a bit of professional wrestling, so he fancied himself as the protector of the crew. He would see to it that they survived all situations. He was all muscle controlled by a fair amount of brains.

Willy's lament drew his attention. He took off one evening in the water taxi. He ran through a woman's backyard, took the clothes-line on the run, bundled it up, and brought it all back to the ship.

"O.K., Willy" he said, "Sort it out. Plenty of sheets now, and stuff the pillow cases with the extra stuff. Fix up the bunks. Towels, and so forth, we can use too. Anyone putting on the tit-holders gets thrown overboard. Get going!"

He took the silk panties, climbed up the rope ladder to the crew's nest, and attached them to the height. They flew out in the breeze.

"That's the flag of our future!" he shouted to us below. The crew cheered. So now we had a flag too! IT became the talk of the Harbor.

Now the ship stood out more than ever. Only ship in the Harbor amid various sailing and motor water craft of smaller dimensions. Strange ship, unpainted, with rope ladders going up to the cross arms of the two masts, a row of large portholes on the bridge facing forward like eyes watching the world. It had metal tube railings around the superstructure to save the crew from falling off into the sea. Dominating it all was a barrel-like crow's nest on the forward mast, made of rounded metal tubing…it could safely hold a drunken lookout. (but what Captain could tolerate one?) In large bold white letters the high bow proclaimed: "FLYING KATE." On the glassy waters of Wilmington Harbor, which was actually a parking lot for boats surrounded by an industrial area, it appeared to be just a tramp of the sea.

People going by in the water taxi wondered about the ship. We who were aboard her did the same. What was to be her destination? The Captain's Dream? The San Pedro waterfront wanted to know too.

The Captain threw a party. He invited people to come aboard. A small spare generator was found below, with its own fuel tank separate from the engine, and it provided electricity for the huge coffee urn, the lights, and some hot plates for a bit of cooking. The galley stove was not presently needed. Matt came aboard and used the urn for tasty cocktails instead of coffee. He cooked up a buffet. Delicious! All sorts of people came…even workers from "The Wilmington Boat Works" nearby. Lamont had some things in mind.

He stood up before the crowd…stately and imposing. They were eager to hear him. People from some of the boats nearby were aboard, and they showed admiration for him in their manner.

"This is a special ship." The Captain informed them. "It was a movie ship. Abe Danches, of the Danches Brothers Production Co. in Hollywood, made a B movie in Alaska with it. He said the movie was 'The Son of Vengeance.' True enough, but the title was actually 'Harpoon.' Erwing Scott wrote the former. They used his script to make the latter. UCLA has the movie in their Archives. No matter. A movie is a movie. But this ship is something! I was below and it has a diesel motor like no other—extremely powerful for the ship. Flying Kate for sure! That's why the heavy planking, twice as thick. A strong ship made to stand the speed it can do. Abe would not tell me where it was built or why. That's his business, I guess. But the ship is my business as its Captain. We are going to run it on the high seas! Even though its size of 104 ft is that of a coastal vessel! Waving palms and sunlit seas beckon us. Lovely girls give beauty to the world. The South Seas were a horror. Now we will make them a joy! Man was not made for war, but perhaps for a life of ease under the trees. I'm getting poetic, so will say it another way. MAN WAS MADE TO LIVE IN A GARDEN. THE FARTHER AWAY HE GOES FROM THAT GARDEN THE GREATER HIS PROBLEMS!!! We are going home!"

The crowd cheered him! It was in their hearts too. Why do you think all those offices have pictures on their walls?

"But gentlemen, the motor is froze up. It will not let us go! Are we to be the victims of a broken dream? Surely not! There are diesel mechanics here who will help us get out to that sea we smell just around the corner from here. Become part of our Dream. We want you. We need you. Your spirit will go with us. You can make those office pictures come true for us and you."

"That's a true sea Captain speaking!" Dirk Caser said, "I will help out."

An old mechanic from the Wilmington Boat Works said he would be over to work on the motor too. He told the gathering that the ship came into the Harbor in 1948 (the year of the movie), and had set for two years...which caused the motor problem.

In casual conversation, Lamont revealed interesting small things about the ship..."The movie company lived aboard the ship in Alaska...that's why the coffee urn for ninety people...the ship has a dark room with large wooden circles on the walls to hold reels of film...many shelves below, too many. Many bunks, too many. My crew will have to remove a lot of it to make room for cargo...hard work for them. We will keep the rugged and rustic appearance of the ship's hull and exterior. It's honest. The entire ship needs mopping and cleanings, and paint on the interior. We will be around for awhile. But always the voyage beckons us."

Well, that Garden concept the Captain got from me. He had said to me that I had some great concepts, and could he use some of them? "Of course Captain, I agreed. Why not?" He did want to make the world better. We were in agreement even on the cosmic level of the spiritual renderings of the mind. More than rapport. Comrades! Comrade sojourners in the country of the mind.

"Teach, but not preach," I said with a bit of inspiration, "Teach positive principles in a negative world. No fables. Man has become an irrational animal living in the mode of ignorance. Look at the present condition of the world. Babylon with atomic triggers! People are living on fables in a smoke and mirrors world. A most dangerous game is being played. Your Command Confidence is positive and needed today, Captain. It's kind, gentle, and loving. It's the wave of the Future. Man was not made for evil, but for good."

"You are my secret weapon," he replied.

"You are inclined to overlook the peccadilloes of your crew." I noted.

"A good enough crew, a good enough crew," he answered. "and your concepts as a writer can be used for good. I will use them. We will fight error together."

Chapter 4

The Captain said he must go ashore again. He was now thinking of how to get fuel and supplies for a voyage. As he left us he said: "Prepare the ship for cargo, then mop up and paint up. We have some paint in the hold."

Our happy residence aboard the ship resolved itself into three weeks of hard work…tearing out shelves, bunks, cabinets, even some fittings in the way of cargo space. Dirk Caser came with an old whale-boat that had a slow chugging motor. We lowered wooden pieces down the side, and kept filling it up. It was hauled ashore somewhere. Too tired to ask. The old mechanic, Bert, went down in the engine room and started working on the motor. We gave him coffee and food, such as we had. Steve slipped him little something at times…some booze and a bit of money. Willy was doing cleaning jobs. Work hard, I told him, the Great U.S. Navy says a clean ship is a happy ship, and our Captain wants to run a tight ship. All of us went to bed so tired we did not hear the sounds of the Harbor anymore…dull thumping ashore, creaking of boats, the taxi bell, horns in distance at night. The sweeping searchlight of the Coast Guard patrol boat came down the channel each night, searching for the dopers.

We asked Caser where he was from. "I live on the San Pedro waterfront." He did not say where. That was it. He continued to be quite helpful in various ways. He liked to come aboard and talk with Steve in off times. But it never amounted to knowable information for us.

Then it happened. We ran out of food.

"That bastard Capone is living on our money," Steve yelled, "Let's go see him!"

We did.

He was happy to see us. "You boys come ashore and I will feed you."

Strange thing about Capone. He wanted to feed the world. We would be eating a delicious breakfast at the motel, and he would be standing by the window with a dirty T shirt covering his big belly, and trying to entice the office girls walking by to come in!

"Come in girls, and have some great food." he said thru the screen.

Unknowing, the girls hurried on to work. They were missing better prepared food than the good restaurants were serving. Matt was a food genius! We figured it was his mother's doing, perhaps? But that could only be a small part of it. He had it in the head or somewhere—but it was there! He could have become the chef of a great hotel...with a change of name. We tried to talk with him about it, but he could not see it. His background blinded him. So sad! Matt had learned about the value of using food from the soup kittens of Al. They made Al a "great guy" and provided a spy network that helped keep him alive. For Matt food was the only source of pride he had left. He could take the most ordinary food stuff and make it into an eating delight. His secrets were hidden in unique ways of cooking, lemon juice, shrimp sauce, and herbs and spices. Rather than gangster, we were starting to think: "Good ole Matt, the cook."

But not Steve. He was angry about our money for ship's use, some of which had become Matt use. He had just shot a seagull that had crapped on him from the rigging above the deck. It fell into the water alongside. My pistol! Then he told us he was going ashore to kill Matt!

"Not with my revolver," I said, "There's not enough money involved to do the ship much good anyway, and he did get us a ship."

Steve cooled down reluctantly.

Ted shook his head about the matter, and then talked about how great things had become for us. He had something to say. "You know the office girls in our hometown dream about adventure in their lonely rooms at night. The working guys are too tired for it, and lay on their backs and snore away the night...but they dream of it some during the day. The wheelers and dealers who plot procedure to make more money are too busy...but they look at those pictures in the offices and do dreaming too. (I had mentioned that to Ted and he caught the vision of it) Here we are right in the lap of Lady Adventure! It's not a neat lap, but a dramatic one! Most men just flirt with her, but we dove right into her lap! Exciting! We have really got something here!"

We cheered his speech.

Groceries came aboard from a warehouse that supplies stores. "Just God taking care of his crew." I said.

Near dusk we sat on deck with cups of coffee watching the Industrial Harbor. It never ceased to amaze us. So alive! There were small boats moving in to anchor at floating drum buoys. Large boat cranes reared up aft like metal giants. A huge metal forest of oil derricks was in the background. Dull bangings came from a nearby shipyard. Black smoke was rising up in a column near the cranes.

Night was not without its odd happenings. Dope was being used. We felt the bump of a boat against the side of our ship. Looking down, there was a long-haired guy, naked and blonde, stretched out and crying. "Get going!" Steve shouted at him. He had one oar, and worked his boat toward a long white yacht nearby we knew was abandoned. He climbed aboard it for the night. About that one! A lone rich guy had been bringing a new woman aboard every night. And they would whoop it up for awhile. But one night there was a hell of a noise aboard! Steve said he must be raping her. But later we found he was trying to do something unnatural to her, and she was smashing him around with a chair! The next night he came aboard bandaged up like an Egyptian mummy. Then he disappeared. The hospital was our guess. Well, Mr. Long-hair brought three of his buddies during the day and they took up happy residence in his boat. One full moon night, they all stood naked on the deck and howled at the moon! The Harbor had things going on in it. Our Captain would not even allow smoking ordinary cigarettes or drinking (except at parties, which were few)-we were to run a clean and tight ship. We are not bums, druggies, or criminals, the Captain told us—we are adventurers! And we agreed. Let the nights be for sleeping and our days for adventure.

Someone stole our skin boat. It was hanging alongside under our little crane arm. Of no water use really. Just a prop left over from movie. That movie! We did dream some about the beautiful women that must have slept in our bunks. Could not life have kept a few of them aboard? We would have treated them in a royal manner. The Captain would have demanded it. We jokingly brought this up with Matt. His comment was: "You boys are horny. Better hurry, and get you out to the islands."

A mystery. There were seven bright Jap flags painted on the bridge! What about this? No one knew. Those flags said the ship had shot down that many Jap planes. How could this be? Dirk Caser knew…but we had no idea that he did know.

"We need some money to keep going." Steve said, "Let's get some."

We parked the car across the channel. At night, Steve got on the raft alongside the ship. (another prop of the movie) I lowered a bag of copper fittings down to him. Ted started to lower a bull rope down that was used for dockings. It was so heavy the raft began to sink. "Take it back up!" Steve said. At the stern there was a medical cabinet attached to the cabin wall outside…which had medical supplies and even shiny instruments for minor surgery. But we thought it might be needed, so we left it alone. However, a large locker on the stern yielded some things of value. We put things in a bag. Steve and I set out across the channel, just paddling away slowly.

Near the middle of the channel, we saw the searchlight of the patrol ship. She was coming right for us, and passed close, not seeing us down on the water so low. Her light was off to the side on the anchored boats. Close call.

We reached the mud flats on the other side. They were extensive with the tide out. Damn! But Steve, with his big boots on, said for me to grab the bags and get up on his back. He was indeed strong. We made it to the car O.K. with the loot.

The fittings were on the scale at a buying place. The man said to us, "You boys did not steal this stuff did you?"

"We are just changing the ship to haul cargo." Steve gave the reply.

"Who should I make out the bill of sale to?"

We gave Al's Prairie Ave address in Chicago, and a similar name. We were failures as criminals. A direct paper trail. But it was too petty affair to go anywhere. Who did we rob?

Chapter 5

The long days of work were broken by brief visits to places ashore that were of some interest to the crew. That vast stretch of oil fields out in the distance was strange in our sight and a challenge. We found it to be a maze of roads and machinery, with its towers reaching the sky. Dirty men worked in it like monkeys in a forest. The heavy smell of oil permeated all that was there. Here was the black gold that turns the engine of the world. Here the Harbor and its many boats seemed remote. Was this place in California, the Golden Land?

Bert invited us to visit the Wilmington Boat Works. Here the promise of the sea reigned supreme. Men's dreams were being fashioned out of wood. It's sweet smell mingled with the smells of resins and paints. Bert guided us around a sleek boat being built. It was not like "The Flying Kate." No boat was like our ship. He told us that our ship was of great interest to him. He said he was getting somewhere with our motor, but it would bear the scars of standing so long. He said that people there considered our ship a mystery. "Boats are built strong here," Bert informed us as we left the Works, "The winter storms are fierce around here." The workers regarded us with interest because of that ship out there in their Harbor. Perhaps they thought we were movie people come back to make another one?

The Captain informed us that Marie Shrimp was located in San Pedro with a new EATERY. I took the crew to see her place. It was like the old one. Feed the sea folk was her thing. She had the big EATERY sign up.

"Marie," I said in joke, "You need to marry Capone and you can feed the world together. He can really cook!"

"I'll stay away from him!" she retorted, "He would have me running a whore-house in no time at all!"

"That never was his thing. It was Al who gave the girls a "home". Matt is just a moron who calls morons maroons. Now he is becoming a rather nice moron. You should trade cooking secrets with our cook."

"I'll pass for now."

Marie set the crew down, and gave them a hot meal.

"You boys look hungry. Surely the Captain isn't starving you?"

"No" Ted replied, "That's just our natural look. We are surviving the Harbor."

"It's a hell of an exciting place, isn't it? This waterfront goes around a long ways. It's my kind of place to be. And the Captain is it's shining star! We must throw a party sometime."

"The Captain already did one, but aboard ship." Ted said.

"We need to have a sea folk party on the waterfront too." Marie mused. "I'll set up one that will knock their rudders off. We should give the Captain a place where he can sparkle."

"Do it Marie," Steve urged.

"Need to save up some bucks for it first." Marie promised, "Let's make it a voyage one."

Steve wanted to make another run across the channel. After the close call with the raft we decided against that. So we looked around. We saw a boat on the deck of the yacht the hippies were sleeping on.

"Let's get it!" Steve said.

At night we paddled the raft quietly over to the yacht. Up on the deck, we put a rope on the boat and swung it over the side. It came back and struck the side. There was a boom like a big drum. Failure as criminals again. The hippies awoke from their dope, and came running out like an ant nest disturbed. They did not want to mix with Steve who was ready to throw them overboard. People in the area did not want to get involved with anything happening at night. Some lights did show on some boats.

We got the boat on the water, went back to our ship, and loaded another bag. We made a run back across the channel to the mud flats. Then took the boat back to the yacht. The hippies had come out hollering when disturbed. But Steve could holler louder: "Pull the damn boat up, or we will come aboard and evict you." They complied. "You guys really stink from bad smoke." Steve told them.

Suddenly the Captain showed up at the ship in a motor launch. He told us to get in. We went down the channel around San Pedro to the Rancho Palos Verdes area. Moored the launch at a dock, and walked across the road to a large house up on a hill. It had a commanding view of the Pacific Ocean.

Inside the house the Captain said to us: "Meet Mr. Foxberger."

He was an older energetic man used to giving orders. "Sit down. I want to have a look at the Captain's crew." he said. He turned to Lamont. "Yes, they look fine."

"Mr. Foxberger owned some ships and was in the shipping business here. He thinks we might haul frozen swordfish from South America." The Captain informed us. "We would have to put in refrigeration in the hold."

"Expensive. And short supply would be a problem too. But they pay high for swordfish steaks." Foxberger summed up. It would be a risky venture to start with.

We had heard an option.

Being right under the belly of L.A., the Captain was approached by the Drug Trade.

"Big money, Captain." The man said.

"We are not murderers of men." Lamont informed him. "Never come near any of us again, or the F.B.I. will be notified."

He told us about it, and had something to say. "These are the days of Perfidious Malarkey. Evil mischief is afoot. The good ole boys network is almost as bad as the bad ole boys network. Corruption reigns due to the five deadly passions men love so well. I want my crew to overcome them…namely Anger, Lust, Greed, Attachment to material things, and Vanity. Being a tight ship means a yogi ship. Meditation is a method. We will establish a good routine. Why will you do this? Because you love me, as I love you my crew." Steve and I were hanging our heads a bit. Capone too. Willy was on the edge. Ted was thinking carefully.

A surprise came. Men arrived to install a refrigeration unit for ship use---paid for! Who? The Captain did not know. A mysterious benefactor! We had the forward hold cleared, cleaned, and painted just in time. The unit went in and waited for the motor to start up. Capone was delighted. We would have better food. Matt had organized the galley, and had cleaned up the galley stove spick and span. The rest of the ship was being done up proper by us. We would have us a nautical little world out on the sea. Our Captain was happy about it all slowly taking good ship shape.

"Next thing," Steve said, "He will be asking us to pray."

"It will come." I said. "We have a truly good Captain. He believes in Law and order just as God does. Only the real evil-doers like Babylon."

Bert was working below on a sunny day. Suddenly the motor roared into life!!! A big black cloud of smoke blossomed at the stern. The crew cheered! It was our great day! The Captain came aboard, and walked the deck up and down in much glee. He was ready for a voyage on the high sea. He allowed us a few cocktails on the stern that evening. Capone made sandwiches that must have come down from the heaven that men dream about. We wondered what he had put on them? (it was shrimp sauce) The Captain praised Matt to the crew. Our cook was ecstatic. He had become worth something to something to someone in the world! The Capone background was fading. (but memories must always remain)

On the dock a white mid-sized dog came up to us. He had a black nose, bright eyes, flop-over ears, a long bushy tail, and appeared to be starving. A Heinz 57 breed of dog. It was obvious someone had left him for good on the dock. The Captain came to a stop. The dog came to him wagging his tail wildly.

"I will not allow any living creature to starve in my presence," our Captain stated, "Take 'Sporty' aboard the ship and feed him. We will keep him."

"Sporty" looked like my childhood dog long gone. "I picked him up, held him like baby, and put him in the water taxi as it came up to the dock.

Getting him aboard was not easy. It is a difficult climb up a wiggly rope ladder with wooden boards for steps. I put a large towel under his belly, roped him up, and he was swung out over the water and lifted up on to the deck. He was scared, but happy. He ran crazy all over the ship…a new world.

"Well now," Steve said, "We got us a practical creature aboard. His psychology is if you can't eat it, or screw it, pee on it. That's more sense than a lot of people have."

Sporty proved him wrong right off. He was licking Capone's hand, and Matt was getting ready to cry. The big question is, did Sporty know Matt was the cook? Anyway, we had a new member of the crew.

Matt stayed ashore most of the time in the Harbor. He was a landlubber at heart. Chicago, you know. The gangs were too busy killing and making money to go near the Lake. Lake Michigan is similar to the sea. Boats in Chicago were alien to the gangsters. Miami was different. Matt came aboard only to visit his galley and do work on it. When he did, he would needle the crew a bit. He always told the crew they were horny. This notion amused him.

"You boys are horny! You will get worse eating my good food. You need a hot whore! I should go around the bars and look for one for you. Ask the Captain if you can have one." Matt concluded with a snicker.

Steve hit him hard. "We will get a goat aboard for you, Matt. Remember how the cows around Chicago were too high up and slippery? Messy too. The goat will have some handles for you to hang on to when you mount up."

"Now you boys show some respect!" Matt said getting angry.

When the Captain did overhear something like this he said kindly: "You demean yourselves by talking the low mental stuff."

He was becoming the crew's anchor in port on the dark Ocean of Life. Out on the sea, the Captain would become The Law. His directives would have to be obeyed. His noble intention was to have the crew discipline itself from within.

Captain Lamont was invited to the bars and clubs around the area—even to those in Long Beach and the city of L.A. Many wanted to meet him. He was becoming a legend. It was the same as in Chicago. The crew was hoping that soon now a viable offer would be made that might produce a profitable cargo.

Chapter 6

Bert kept coming aboard. He had informed the Captain of his service in the U.S. Navy during the first World War, and of his nautical life thereafter. He was a sea oriented person. He had a private conversation with our Captain.

"Captain Lamont, I did service in the U.S. Navy during the first great war...and have always worked in the nautical world. I want to die at sea and be buried in it...and I'm dying now. The doctors tell me it will be soon. I want to come with you. Take care of your motor too. It's going to remain a smoker."

"I understand your position and your desire. I agree with you. You can come with us. I will keep your secret." Lamont said kindly. He had strong liking for the old man. He thought of Lenora being in the sea.

Bert responded by putting his talents to work right off. He was an expert in the constructing of gimbals on bunks for comfort at sea. This would allow the sleeping place to hold to the horizon despite the motions of the ship.

"I'll make your sleeping pads clouds you can dream on," he said to the crew. "You will thank me when there are storms at sea."

He did not stop there. He built a dog-house for Sporty at the stern, with a peaked roof to run water off into the scuppers. He made the bottom of it to float on gimbals too! And he made an area in the corner of the stern where Sporty could do his wastes over the scuppers...so a bucket of water could be pulled up from the sea and wash the waste down the scuppers. Sporty was a bright dog, and learned the procedure quickly. "Sporty is now a sea dog like me." Bert let us know.

Dirk Caser came aboard with the Captain. They called a meeting of the crew around the table, and coffee was served by willing Willy.

The Captain did not take over. Dirk Caser did.

"This is a C.I.A. ship!" he said.

We sat in stunned silence.

"I want my money back!" Steve bellowed. The rest of us agreed to that. We did not intend to get involved in any war…here…there…or anywhere. We were focused on the lush islands of dreams.

The Captain pondered the situation quickly and spoke up. "Dirk did not tell me what this meeting would be about. I though he had a cargo option for us. This is a surprise to me too! Well, we do not have any viable economic prospects, my crew. Dirk, what do you have in mind? My crew will not participate in any hurting or killing."

"Operation Goodheart! You all want an adventure. This is the greatest one you will ever have in this world. We are going to establish Democracy in Costa Rica. It has become a vital necessity to your government. You will be doing a great service to your country. We were watching your Captain for some time, and we need you as the hometown boys out on a lark. There will be no hurting or killing involved. WE are most happy that your Captain is not kosher. The spy system does not consider him to be a Captain at all. He has no papers! Nor do any of you as future seamen. And you have a ghost ship! It has been put fully under cover. The spy system does not take a movie ship serious. No one does! Abe has acted within our circle of operations over the years…and has been able to make his movie too. The movie is an excellent cover! Records and papers have either been eliminated or obscured. Hardly anyone knows where our ship was built or why or where it will finally end up. It will be scrapped after this Operation is terminated."

The ship's future made the Captain look sad. He loved the ship, and his crew. But there was still the voyage to come…

Now speculation ran rife. Dirk Caser would not confirm any of it. He only gave us what was needed to influence our acceptance of Operation Goodheart. Did Matt get a phone call directive to get the Captain to the Circle Club? (for a fee?) He was dead broke…and he had a lot of practice at keeping his mouth shut. Abe at the circle Club? The Captain? No, not in character at all. At what point? When? Where? Why? The C.I.A. never says. Secret are its working ways. It is authorized to act international only…but it is partners with the F.B.I. authorized to act within the U.S.…and it secretly acts where it needs to do so. Since no one knows, even within the organization, it is not possible to figure out anything. Anyway, we were within its hands now.

"WE need your promise not to write or expose anything regarding this matter—until 2000!" Dirk said.

"That's a lifetime." I objected.

"Do you want to harm your country?"

"You have the promise. The Fleet Marine Force is in my background.

"WE know all about you," Dirk said. "Everyone of you."

"We have a Sea Change!" the Captain said to sum it up. "It can work out well. Now we have a good motive for the voyage. Better than money, girls, and easy living. Those are not noble goals. Democracy has excellent hopes in it for people to become better and live better."

"You talk like a politician trying to get elected to an office." Steve said.

"I am running for office." Lamont revealed, "It's the Heart. When Dirk named it Operation Goodheart, he got me involved."

Dirk had more to say (unusual for the C.I.A.), but he thought it was germane for our strong motivation and had been decided previously by higher ups. It was on need to know basis, and would be on the back burner for many years. He seemed willing to speak rather freely. I suspected he was going with us.

"To the south of our continent there are malignant forces at work. Argentina is going Fascist. Other countries south of Costa Rica are developing criminal cartels to smuggle in drugs on us. Small dictatorships are coming up like mushrooms. In Nicaragua rebel forces are threatening Costa Rica…they even have camps in over the border right now! There are people in Costa Rica trying to establish a Democracy. We are going to help them do it. This will amount to a cork in the bottle-neck, just like the Marines at Guadalcanal. We are striving to be free, and keep back the forces that won't let others be free. The game is playing chess with countries. Costa Rica's does not have an Army! There we will help develop a militia or Police Guard Force to put out local fires. We have two of the latest U.S. fighter planes at our call to bring balance to any military situation."

"Yes," Steve interrupted, "What are those seven jap flags painted on the bridge for? How did they get there?"

"Something for you to be proud of…this ship shot down that many enemy planes in the Big War. It is a hidden story. The Japs had a biological lab hidden in the jungle amid the islands. Our planes were unable to find it. A ship had to go in fast, bombard the building, and mark it out for the planes. 'The Flying Kate', considered just a tramp boat, fooled the Jap with its speed. It was loaded with guns and expert gunners. On coming out from the raid, they attacked us. They lost seven planes. A few bombs did come near. You should have smelled the cordite in the air! We had us a joke about it. There was a saying that Roosevelt said he hated war, but loved the smell of gun-powder. This one is for Roosevelt, our crew said."

"You sure are full of surprises." Ted noted.

"And of instructions, too—and they must be followed closely. Your Captain will remain the Law at sea, but I will be the Law behind him. Actually, your Government will be running this Operation through its secret Agency. You will go to the Marine Base to take training. It will be a repeat for one of you here. He can tell you how nice it is—and how it saved his life when the going got rough. But there should be no shooting this time. Yet you must be able to defend yourselves. There are always risks, you know. Unforeseen happenings can occur. It's behind the scenes, but violent men will be around. You will be there as the Peace Corps workers…always a good cover. There are now ample funds for fuel and supplies, and monies for personal use. Steve will not have to kill Capone. Bert and Capone are not to know any specifics, as we even keep those from you, and give out generalities. They think I am a secret benefactor of your dream of adventure. Bert was paid to work the motor by me. Capone got a little loot too in secret. Feed the boys, I told him. He understands hidden corruptions. On board he will think I am out to capture the show…He suggested I throw the captain overboard at sea. Brother Al's ghost must be roaming around here. At sea both of these men will finally figure it out. Meantime we can keep them from talking on land.

"You are a sneaky guy." Willy said.

"Comes with the job, Willy. But it is for a good use this time."

"At least we are not losing our money." Steve said.

"Do not take any money from groups or individuals. Use our money only. It can be the root of all evil, you know. Proper procedure requires that you stay away from people, and keep your mouth shut. Never answer questions. At ports just float in and out fast. Always move fast. At the Marine Base no one will know anything about you. The officers will be curious. Let them remain so. If you get mad at a D.I., and you will, KEEP YOUR MOUTH SHUT! Take what comes, and profit by it. There's more. You will have no radio at sea. It will be up to your captain to keep you alive at sea. You will not contact any ship. You will avoid them by your speed. No communication whatsoever. Just out distance them. They will think you a tramp running some stuff. No big deal. In port, you will not discuss the ship or any of your doings. Just let your money do the talking. Most will accept that. Leave port immediately after fuel and supplies are aboard. Let them think they saw you. MOVE! No bars. No clubs. No socializing. No government contacts. Above all, no women! They are favorite spy tools. There are spies everywhere. Don't think you are better than the pros. You are not. You are just amateurs. SILENCE is your best defense. Pretend to be smugglers by the appearance of your ship, and your unwillingness to talk. Since you are not doing dope or drinking we can trust you. I realize we are asking a lot of young bucks, but a lot is at stake…and Capone tells me you are horny. Remain so. No, it's his joke mostly. Time is a weapon we have learned to use well. It is effective when there are many ramifications to something. They disappear in time. That is why we have your promise to the year 2000. WE want the ship to be a ghost ship until then at least…there are ramifications involved. There are those who would sink your ship at sea…if they become aware of its purpose and mission."

Chapter 7

The Captain ordered a trial run of the ship. It responded well to the rudder after the anchor was hauled. We headed down the channel, around San Pedro, and out to sea. Waves were running moderate under a bright sun. The crew was captivated by the sea they had dreamed about so long. Land was falling away behind us. The world became sea and sky married in a vast circle. The ship became a small world in the middle of it. The Captain hit the motor up hard to check the speed out. There was a dark plume of smoke behind the ship for some distance. The speed did not satisfy him.

"We need to visit the dry-docks. Our speed has been compromised. The bottom has growth. She needs to be scraped, and painted with an anti-fouling coating. A sleek bottom will give us the speed we need." He informed the crew.

Bert took over. He knew the Ways and ways. "The Flying Kate" was hauled up on the Ways, and the growth of years sitting was seen. The Captain did an inspection, talking to the crew as he walked the ship around. He was in a highly happy mood.

"I love this ship! It is special. I could not have a better one built. See how the deep V under the high prow moves back and goes flat at the stern. At slower speeds we can take the heavy seas well and at faster the stern will step up to go. Special design!" Lamont informed his crew. "I wanted all of you to see and know the bottom of the ship. If anyone of you have to take the helm, he will know how to run the ship. What you don't know can kill you. Knowledge is the power to save lives, to make right decisions, and to run things the right way. Each of my crew must learn seamanship. We will depend upon each other."

Bert nodded his head in approval.

We were taken to a remote corner of the USMC Pendelton Proving Grounds…by private white van. This area is 40 miles across. Tanks were seen moving around. The thumping of heavy weapons came to our ears. Always an active military place here. We were to have 6 weeks of special forces training to handle civil and military control in formative and unstable conditions. The Marine officers had a D.I. for us…a hard one. (is there any other kind?)

"Get the hell out of that van—and line up!" he yelled at us. Willy was scared, Capone was confused, Ted was interested, Steve sneered, and I thought…not again? The Captain took his place in line with us. I did not quite know what he was thinking—but I knew he wanted a tight crew to run a tight ship…and I knew he was going to get it…and it too.

"Damn," the D.I. lamented, "What kind of crap am I getting out here?"

He was not in the know. The Marine officers thought they were. They had been told we were to help in protecting the President when he left the White House for a relaxing spot. Strange looking guys for secret service use. They shrugged their shoulders. Orders were orders. Comply. One thing they were not going to interfere with the D.I.—and he was out for blood. That's the way the Marine Corps is. I was weary. Anyway, I thought, it would not be The Fleet Marine Force this time. But all D.I.'s are wearing. They are ego—killers. It's a wearing down process.

The Marine Corps mentality is delivered thru the D.I.'s:::stand up and keep your mouth shut. Do the drill…do the drill…do the drill. That rifle is your best friend. Shoot first and shoot straight. The USMC is founded upon the rifle. They train you to whip it around on the march in deep sand and on the Parade Ground…all the same…better not ever be out of line with it. We were given rifles.

"It has fire in it," I told Willy. "Wait until the firing range comes up."

Basics first: Sleep in tent. Out! Exercise with the rifle overhead. Eat slop. Capone was horrified…but wisely he remained silent. The Syndicate was not the only organization that had tough people. His big belly got sore. Run the obstacle course. He was out of shape…lay and groan…"God dammit, get up and get going or I'll give you something hard to do!" The D.I. hollered in his ear. He got up. Willy started to cry. "OOOoooo What do we have here? A baby!" the D.I. exclaimed in disdain. He did not spare any of us his nasty comments. We all got it. (no one wants it) In the tent, flat on the cot, Willy wailed, "They are trying to kill us." Lamont took it all in stride, and I could see the D.I.

looking strangely at him at times. Steve threatened to punch the D.I. out. It was a mistake. Ted just suffered quietly. We were a sorry crew.

But then the sore stuff started to heal, and the inner pride began to develop. The crew were becoming survivors. They would go away with a valuable asset in life. Some of the command confidence of the Captain was getting into his crew. He noted it, and was happy about it. This business was saving the Captain a lot of work on the ship. There would be a good start to the voyage.

After the basics, we got out of the hands of the D.I., and the tactics of the special forces were taught in a number of sessions to complete the weeks.

One officer got Willy aside once. "What is the President like?" he asked.

Willy went into a blank look.

Finally, back at the ship, the Captain informed us we would stand muster and keep up the exercise drill…every day of the voyage. Keep in shape was his command. We agreed.

Capone was getting suspicious.

"What is this all about?" he wanted to know.

"We have to please our benefactor," the Captain told him.

"Screw him!" Matt replied.

"No money." Lamont stated flatly.

During off times in port we would question Matt about brother Al. He was willing to let us know that Al was "a good guy." Our curiosity never died out. It was a sort of idle pastime for us.

"My brother gave farms girls homes in the whore-houses; he put up soup kitchens for the poor people in the cities; he gave his family plenty of money to live on; he paid thousands of dollars for flowers so those killed would have a nice funeral; he saw to it that there would be a lot of nice marble memorials on graves in Mt. Carmel; he took special care of his kid brother; he was generous to those who gave support to his empire. Mama always complained to Al about 'blood money, blood money'…but when he took her out of the old brick house on Prairie Ave and put her into luxurious quarters she cooled down, and got to like the good living. He was always nice to the ladies. If they were acting up, he would say 'do you want me to find you a better home?' He was a gentleman. He was worth $100,000,000 in 1937! When you are at the top, you got guys trying to knock you off it. Bunch of crafty bums tried to kill him. Al got them first!"

"He did send the most famous Valentine ever," Ted said sardonically, "It made him the most known citizen of the U.S. worldwide."

"Those bums deserved it!" Matt let us know.

"It was Al's undoing too." Ted said. "It got the Feds attention."

"It was his men who were nasty." Matt continued, "They wrote the story of Chicago in red with the 'Chicago typewriter.' Al always said it was a disgrace to be killed with a cheap gun. He bought the best. Had a dozen Thompson Sub-Machine Guns....those with the drums full of 45 slugs. His men used to complain they were too heavy, and would climb up on firing...hard to keep them horizontal...fire in short bursts, Al told them. He made the Thompson Co. and they admitted it too. Al said a man should go out in style, and be covered with flowers afterward. He like flowers a lot. Those guns would make swiss cheese out of cars and the bums in them. Al liked his guns. But then the bums started using them too. You know how it is. So Al would shoot first. We just got the same instruction at Camp."

"Different shootings for different reasons." Steve said. "The USMC protects your ass."

"I felt good in the khaki uniform." Matt reflected.

"The Captain will continue you in it." Ted said.

Dirk Caser was as curious about me as I was about his ship. "It was the Marine Corps all over again, was it not?"

"Hell no, time changes everything. Marine thinking stays the same because it's up front stuff. The Navy has to make its soldiers of the sea hard, lean, and mean. It's a special thing. I would rather not live that way. Those who do like it can do it. They deserve everyone's respect, and they get it. The USMC is needed by the people of the U.S. more than ever today. It will be sorely needed yet. Back in time we were dumped in the Jap's lap on Guadalcanal. The Navy ran away because of the planes. That Green hell on the equator is a survival place. There it was our personal survival and that of the U.S. too. Henderson Field was the key to the whole war out there. The Japs came back with all their best—to get it back at all costs. We had to dig in, and live like scared rats. Every free citizen walking the streets owes the Marine Corps for their freedom bought with blood in the mud. The Japs were head-choppers with their swords. Combat Marines can never be civilians again. The gap will always be there. What the hell does the young guy walking the street know? He does not even care. He's focused on women and making money, and perhaps some dope too. The vets are just history to him. That's how it goes. At the San Diego Base I saw a few hundred Marines graduate from boot camp on the Parade Ground. I hope they never have to experience what we did. Any jungle fighting is mean stuff—especially if it's in a hell-hole like Guadalcanal. Even the natives have a hard time just living there. Do you know what the Japs called it? KA!...the island of death! You have to be there to know...and if you get out of there you are one of the lucky ones. Dirk, keep this ship away from that island!"

"Strange you say that," Dirk revealed, "This was an Army patrol boat, and it was secret under U.S., doing special missions around Tulagi across the way from you Marines. Remember all those small craft plying the waters of Iron Bottom Bay? You probably saw this ship, and never noticed it out there. WE went up the Slot too. The C.I.A. works quiet and hard for the U.S. in many situations never revealed. 'The Flying Kate' was built during the war about 1943, and was used by Danches Bros Movie Production 4 years later to make the B movie 'Harpoon' in Alaska with our O.K....good cover for our ship. They converted the interior to allow the movie company of 26 to live aboard. The movie was released in New Bedford, Mass. In 1948. It was a rough sea adventure made from a rather bad script by Ewing Scott called 'The Son of Vengeance.' The ship was a floating studio. Now you know about that big coffee urn. Had nice women actors aboard. Anyway, you guys won the war out there. The Army and Navy had something to do with it too."

"Just backup. The Marines have to have backup."

"Damn Marines are impossible!" Caser commented.

"That's why we win! Anyway, my fisterous is strong and hard today because of the Marine Corps."

"What's that?"

"Anything you want it to be."

"We need you in the C.I.A. if you are going to talk like that."

Ted painted a sign on Sporty's dog-house. It boldly stated ::: "C.I.A. SEA DOG"

"That's neat," Bert said, "I like your little joke."

"Just wanted to give our dog some class." Ted said.

Bert advised us to visit a shop catering to mountain climbers, and to buy nylon ropes with large clip-ons. He told us there would be heavy seas to navigate, and the clip-ons could go on the metal pipe railings nicely located around our ship. "You need to have Marie make you some leather harnesses too. Get each size and give them to her for the sewings. I do not want to see the waves wash anyone over the side. If you leave the ship during a storm you are a goner. Stay alive! Sporty has to have the same deal."

We had a great Captain, and a wise old sea dog to back him up. We were a blessed crew. Dirk remained an unknown in the forming up of the voyage. Capone the cook was a prime asset in the opinion of the crew. Days at sea and working the ship would create the need for food that would not go boring. Food and the bunk are a sea-farer's best friends. But it is the Captain who is central to survival.

The Captain called a meeting of the crew.

"We need to go on a shakedown cruise." He informed us. "Let's visit Cedros island right off the big bay of the Baha. Right on the edge of the Pacific Time Zone, if that means anything to us. We can do some swimming and fishing there."

As our ship headed down the cluttered coast of California, I set up a routine of drinking ginger tea for four days. Sea sickness is a green monster that can't abide the tea. We had Sporty lap up a weak dish of it. He was excited with the new happenings...running around the decks and looking at the sea.

The line of dry mountains on the Baha came up on the port side. The captain kept the ship well off shore for a safer passage and a less visible one. This was to be our navigational modus operandi for much of the voyage near land.

The sea surge was moderate, and the ship rode slow and easy on it. A bright desert sun beat down on water and land. A sea breeze kept us cool. The crew wore hats and dark glasses at the captain's bidding. Being on the deck was a joy. We were doing it! The hometown seemed remote and of another time and world. Even Steve was relaxed and in a good mood. He talked easy with Capone, who had on his dirty T-shirt as always. Delicious smells were coming from the galley. After the meal, Steve lost interest in the cook.

"The Captain may be the Captain," Matt told us, "But I'm the one who is taking care of you boys." he informed us.

"He may be right," the Captain said, "Every man has a bottomless pit."

Steve made a wry smile. "Can't throw the son-of-bitch overboard." he said sadly.

Capone glared at him.

"There must be harmony in my crew." Lamont said, "I'll have you sing a silly song to ruin the day if you do not behave."

"No, not that!" Ted said.

The black plume of destiny was trailing behind the ship. The white wake of destiny was brighter than ever under the plume. "Voyaging, Voyaging, Voyaging!" Walt Whitman was saying. Our Captain was hearing it.

"I heard it is dangerous on the Baha." Willy said.

"Bandits!" the Captain replied. "That's why we will visit Cedros island. It's across a big bay, well away from shore. Remote place. If any boat does come out, it has to go for a long way in our sight first. We are under a mandate to avoid any contact with anyone."

"We have rifles and know how to use them." Steve said.

"Only for direct defense." Lamont reminded him. "Would you want to deny life to any living thing on a beautiful day like this?"

The Captain startled the crew.

"Do I have to kiss you to prove my love? I'm not pretending it. It's more real than the illusion of it in the world."

We had heard something like this somewhere back in time. It seemed to echo the Christ of history.

"No," Ted said, "We know it. We feel it."

"Good!" Lamont said, "And I feel your love returning to me your Captain. It is the way of life on this ship. We are a solid ship.

Multitudes, multitudes are in the Valley of Decision. Many are sailing on the Dark Ocean of Life in leaky ships. They may never reach port...never reach the shining shore."

"Are we on a philosophy cruise?" Ted inquired.

"No, on a real love cruise. We are more fortunate than many in the world. Not only is this the adventure you wanted...but much more than an adventure."

Steve walked to the railing, looking out to sea, trying to figure it all out.

"God is a Spirit." Lamont said, "His spirit gives life to all living things. And the spirit in man moves back to Him. It is the beautiful circle of Truth in love."

"No!" Steve objected, "There is corruption and darkness in it."

"It's only the Snake in the Garden that must be gotten rid of finally." Lamont answered.

A shakedown of the crew was going on too.

The Captain put his arm around Capone. "Our wonderful cook," he said, "Get us some food up on deck and we will celebrate your presence."

Capone started crying, and tried to hide it by walking to the rail. He was remembering telling Dirk to throw the Captain overboard.

The Captain was an example for all of us to start living.

He went into the wheelhouse and took the helm back from Willy, who was getting a lesson in responsibility. Each of the crew would learn the working of the helm. It takes the cooperation of all men to steer a world. Our ship was to be run by all. We had to be an example of Democracy to teach it to others. The Captain was teaching his crew to work things well.

The island proved to be a hot desert place of a moderate size. It was desolate and dry in a hot sun. Swimming off the ship was a delight. The crew shouted and splashed about as if they were back in the swimming hole by the hometown. But here the sun and the vastness of the sea dominated all. Adventure! Our ship looked exciting to us. The Captain dove off the ship to join us. We had become the most fortunate of men. Dirk was remote down here.

Back on deck we had an evening supper on deck amid the splendor of a setting sun. The whole world seemed ablaze with soft red glow. The great orange orb sank slowly in the sea, and left us quiet under the fading light of the afterglow. A perfect day in a remote place had ended.

Up the hook, and start the engine. We set out to make a night run up the forlorn coast so wild and dry. No ship lights came into view. The sea was all ours. We ran on interior lights only.

A wooden ship makes creaking noises. These the Captain listened to and liked. He told us the ship was reading the sea, and telling it back to him. His hand on the helm told him things too. He did not go by paper. He went by the ship and the sea. He hardly ever looked at the compass headings. Willy had frozen on one heading, even though the coast was miles away. We told him "The Flying Kate" was not that fast. But the helm had him scared. We hoped his loose screw was starting to tighten up.

Near daybreak we saw the lights of the Harbor off the starboard side.

Back at anchor we were in a happy mood. All had gone quite well.

The ship and crew were now welded in a working order. The captain gave the O.K. on it and us. We were ready to sail anytime now. He slipped our ship up to a dock smooth and easy, without hitting it. The bull ropes went out to the docking anchors. Supplies and fuel came aboard. The ship was ready for a voyage. Dirk came aboard to plan it out.

Marie Shrimp wanted a sailing party for her Captain. Dirk said No.

The local newspapers in nearby cities informed the public that A Peace Corps Party would be held at the residence of Mr. Foxberger. It was in honor of the Captain, and his Peace Corps workers, who would be going to Costa Rica. They would use their business and administrative skills to improve the functions of the country's government. They would set sail in a Peace Corps ship---"The Flying Kate." Others who could qualify would be able to go on the voyage with them. All organizations should give their support to the noble project.

Dirk said it would be up to him to "dodge out" any do-gooders who showed up for the voyage. He had formulated this interesting ploy as a cover for us, and he would take care of any complications that came up.

The offer in the papers was to allay any suspicions, and it would help make the venture seem kosher. Willy said he was a sneaky one.

Mr. Foxberger lived alone in isolated splendor. The isolated splendor had become a desert island in society for him. He was too alone. He told Dirk to come on with the Party. He wanted some gaiety around the place. "Come and turn my lights on!" he said. He thought the Peace Corps was an excellent solution to the problem of getting the ship going on a voyage, and was sure that good funding was involved. "Excellent!" he said to the Captain, "You look like missionaries rather than businessmen anyway."

Marie took over the house, and Capone went into the kitchen to prepare the foods for the festive launching of the voyage. Many guests came from all over the region. They were mainly curious concerning the Captain. Talk about him always spread like wildfire.

The Captain dressed up, put on his black Homberg hat, picked up his impressive cane, and strode into the crowd to spark them up with sea stories. The stories kept the questions at bay. He was artful in talking all night and saying nothing. He said: "What can you do with a movie ship except use it for a Benefit or go on a Peace voyage with it??? Costa Rica is closer than the islands too. It has beautiful women, beaches, and is tropical too. We have not changed our objective at all. My crew is agreed. So now off we go….." The tea-table ladies all adored him.

Dancing and music was provided outdoors up above the sea. The view was impressive…and passing ships sounded their horns. Foxberger was drinking, and was in a state of euphoria. His big house was ablaze with lights. He too had his admirers.

The table was groaning with all sorts of food made up in new ways. Everyone was going for it like it was the end of eating on earth. Capone put on cleaner clothes, came out, and watched the eaters with approval.

Marie came over and kissed him. "You have greatness in you." she commented.

No regular woman had ever done that to Matt before. Al's women were whores…in the house or out. They were money-orientated. The new feeling made Matt confused, and he was impressed by it…there was more to women than he had thought. He kissed Marie's hand…like in the movies he had seen.

"Damn," Steve blurted out, "Now we got us a Romeo cook, a gangster Romeo cook!!! He may go after us on the voyage."

"Steve, Steve!" the Captain said, "Be kind, gentle, and loving. Capone is trying to become a man. Give him a chance. Do you want to be like Al?"

Capone danced with Marie.

Steve walked away shaking his head.

The ship was tied up at a dock below so people could view it. Rugged, rustic, and ready for the sea. It was not a sanitized ship of the marinas. It was a ship of remote islands and shores beyond the far horizons. A ship of the sea.

The Party lasted long into the night.

THE VOYAGE

Chapter 8

At daybreak the Captain headed the ship down the channel, and out to sea. It was a dull day, and the surf could be heard falling upon the shore. The ghostly cries of the gulls faded away behind us. We were finally on our way into adventure.

Bert and Dirk were talking on stern. Dirk waved his arm back toward California. "Goodbye, La La land." he said. Bert laughed loudly. "It's the Land of many viewpoints, and for some it can be like Alice in Wonderland." "Perhaps we can qualify for being an Alice?" Dirk said in interpretation.

"You look like an Alice," Steve said to him.

"Woo, woo!" Willy sounded.

Then it came. Capone and Bert wanted to know why Dirk was aboard???

"Ask him." The Captain offered.

"This is a C.I.A. ship on a mission for the U.S., and you will hold your silence on this!"

"Come on," Capone replied.

He and Bert looked at Lamont.

"Yes," the Captain replied, "He stands behind me to run the show that no one must know."

"I'm not going to get my ass shot off!" Capone objected.

"No need. It's a peaceful mission. We are bound for Costa Rica to form procedures behind the development there. To tilt the scale in favor of Democratic rule. You will have money, women, and exciting times."

"We will help to establish a Democracy in a Garden paradise. It's a lush land full of flowers and fruits. As always there are snakes in the Garden. We will work to harness the human ones." The Captain revealed. "Costa Rica is a morass of intrigue!"

The ship passed Cedros Island. After over 300 miles of running we passed the bottom of the Baha, and the sea dominated the horizons. Day followed day going south. The motion of the sea surges and washes was countered with the ginger tea-drinkings.

The far line of the Mexican Coast came up to port, and we took to running in closer to save distance down to Costa Rica. We turned off from other ships. We passed Acapulco in the night, and could hear the whoopings up coming from the parties. The port was lit up like a Christmas tree.

Finally we were approaching Nicaragua, with its huge lake near the coast...and beyond the ship moved along the coast of North Costa Rica. Hills and volcanoes dominated the countryside. The immense Gulf of Papagayo had us back out to sea.

It was yet a long stretch of sea to our turning in point around the Cabo Blanco point of the Nicoyo peninsula. Here there was white earth, and white cliffs faced the sea.

Dead ahead there was an isolated sea rainstorm—a black cloud, dropping its dark curtain of rain down to the sea surface.

I got a bucket of water up, some peppermint soap, and soaped Sporty up well. On entering the rain, I shoved him out into it. He was happy in the rain. After the wash, I dried him up with a large towel. He took to leaping over things on deck.

"That soap is burning his behind." Ted said.

"No, look at his happy-face," I replied, "It has given him new life!"

Running up the waters of the long peninsula, we heard the howler monkeys in the trees of the dry forest. We took turns trying to spot them with the binoculars. Olive ridley and Leatherback turtles were burying their eggs in the sands of golden beaches.

Our ship was moving in to dock at the cargo terminal of Punterenas. It was a dismal place of ramshackle docks and buildings all out on a long spit of land. Some fishermen were digging for clams in the mud of the mangroves. We heard some loud music from the spit and sawdust bars. Rustings and rottings. Poor fishing boats tied up at a ramshackle wharf. Driftwood pile-ups. Stench in humid air. Muggy. This was not the place to be. Dirk made a phone call to San Jose.

"O.K., we go up to the head of this long stretch of water to where a river comes into it from the north. There is an uninhabited island up there. Across from it a road comes down near the water. A vehicle geared for the trails, with high clearance, will be there waiting for our use. Mountains come down the starboard side. We will hide the ship in a suitable bay or inlet on this side. Run across in our small boat. Good thing we got a new outboard."

Before leaving the dock, we took a brief walk. We met a drinker. "Come with me." he invited, "I'm going to visit Carmen, our Virgin of the Sea."

"Sorry, I don't know her." Steve said, "What bar does she hang out in?"

We were able to run the ship into a hidden spot, and in sight of the island. Bert and Sporty were to stay on board and guard the ship. The setting was dramatic.

On the opposite shore we met an unkept man living in a cracker box house on the trail. He had been paid a few dollars to watch our vehicle, which appeared to be a military type. He was out to warn us about a local danger.

"There is a witchy woman on that island out there. At midnight she turns into a huge monkey. She haunts drunks and men out cheating on their wives. Better watch it!"

"Don't talk about my wife that way." Ted told him.

"What name do you have?" Dirk asked.

"It is Juan." Juan said.

"Everybody in the country is named Juan." Dirk replied.

"That is true." he agreed.

"How the hell do you manage to live out here?"

"I have a spring, and do some farming, and fish up above that island. The river brings food down to the Gulf...and the fish come. I manage."

"O.K. Juan, we are sport fishermen. We have a ship across the way up in an inlet. There is an old man aboard. We want you to look in on him at times to see that he is O.K. Call a doctor for him if he gets ill. He is a good guy. Knows the sea. Can give you some good information to use yourself. Trade some stories. Take care of our boat. It is tied up by yours at that flimsy dock. We will pay you for what you do. We will be in San Jose."

"I know the inlet well. It is a nice place for a ship to anchor. I will bring your old man some fresh fruit. What is his name?"

"It's Bert."

We ran the vehicle around the head of the Gulf, and took off down the pot-hole highway to San Jose some 50 miles distant. To the north, the Arenal Volcano had a glowing cloud at its summit, and was blasting house-sized rocks 1000 ft in the air. It was a cone volcano, and known as one of the most active in the world.

"Let's visit that Volcano." Willy said.

"Later on." Dirk promised.

The road climbed up to 4000 ft, and there was the great bowl of Valle Central, the heart of Costa Rica—with the grid-city of San Jose in the middle of it. A ring of volcanoes dominated the perimeter of the Central Valley. Smokers above the green uplands. Cloud mantles covered the uplands. Neat rows of dark green shiny-leafed coffee bushes were everywhere.

The land was rolling, forested and farmed. Small farms, grassy meadows, pine forests, and poverty. Flame trees of the Royal Poinciana appeared like exploding bombs, here and there, on the hillsides. Flowers were everywhere. The Captain took special delight in the many varieties of orchids. Colorful farm towns and small cities surround the capital. All was paradisiacal, and in sharp contrast to the sleazy port below. But amid the flowers there was poverty.

San Jose was wooden and adobe buildings, narrow streets, many pot-holes, shady parks full of flowers—a three mile stretch of streets divided into barrios. Historic buildings of colonial aspect were few and downtown. In the northwest area there were hard-luck whores, drunks, and those who had been struck foul balls in the game of life. Shabby hotels offered rice and beans for meals.

"It's still a Paradise because of its garden atmosphere." The Captain commented.

"Your Paradise gets smokings and shakings at times." Dirk informed him. "But the people have a wonderful climate and a lush land so they persist and survive. The coffee bean is the King here. But as for power, there are many factions contending here."

The University was in the better part of town. Dirk drove us to take up residence in the area. Ted, having been a school teacher, was happy about the location. We were to be installed like new plumbing in the intellectual life...to help the flow of power run to a Social Democracy. Most would think us to be "Peace Corps" administrators. Dirk advised us to so talk, act, and do on the surface.

Steve wanted to know about the girls. Out on the streets he saw them. Tall dark-haired young women with beautiful bodies. Dark eyes sparkling. The climate was healthy. Few cars, trucks, or factories. Warm days and cool nights. Fresh fruit and vegetables. The gypsy beauty of Spain had come through the Pioneers to a good place. The girls wore gaily colored dresses to fit their good mood. Enticing! Steve found them friendly.

"O.K.," Dirk said to us, "Anyone who gets out of line gets exiled to Chira Island. That's where the monkey woman is. You know, Ted's wife."

"I'll behave" Willy promised us.

"I don't have the galley stove here to allow Willy his daily looks at the fire." Matt said half joking. "He may set something."

"No fire!" Willy said. "But I want to visit volcanoes."

"Throw him in." Steve said.

I was hoping that all the news events would be in the direction of a Social Democracy.

Dirk called a meeting in a back room of the conference area.

"Our function is to be spark plugs in the motor of development here. Ted gets assignments out in the field pertaining to the school system development. Steve will work in the Police Guard Militia. John goes to Public Relations. Mr. Capone is here under a different profile and a new name...necessary so as not to excite friends and enemies about any power play. He can help in food production. Willy we will put in charge of forest fires...no, no, no. How about metal working? Our main function is to support a man called Don Pepe. He is political and a great leader toward Democracy. Our objective is to make the 1949 Constitution work in the land. It is a copy of the U.S. Government.

There has been an execution or two in the past. Had to eliminate hard-noses. Most of the would be dictators were exiled. Now some are trying to come back via the rebels here and in Nicaragua. Rebels have established a few camps across our border in the wild and remote area to the north. We want more school teachers than policeman in this country—as our main weapon for the future. We will support the National Liberation Party. The surrounding small countries are all dictatorships. We want Costa Rica to be in the midst of them as an example of right functioning government for the good of all people. There are a few coffee barons left who are with us. They do not want civil wars or rebel disruptions to the economy to obstacle the Coffee Trade. These are reasonable requests."

"What will our immediate procedure be for now?," Ted wanted to know.

"Go out into the field. Look around. Get ideas. Think to the objective, then work to establish functional procedure in concrete action. When you have something going, then turn it over to others to develop. Start more action elsewhere."

"Are we members of the C.I.A.?" Steve asked.

"Certainly not." Dirk said, "I'm your contact, and we work with circumstances and others toward objectives. The USMC is for front line direct defense. The C.I.A. is the hidden hand to protect the power of the U.S. in the international world. We keep The Silence like the Syndicate, but for different reasons. We are for Power. The Syndicate is for Profit, and that for individuals. Actually all the lash-ups of man are for money…money is behind them all! It is the root of all evil, as they say. We try to make it different. Circumstances can cause us to change our procedures where needed. Here we are out to establish a Democracy for the good of all…always remember this."

Weeks went by. We slowly got the feel of things. The people were gentle, kind, and loving. The Captain took to them like a duck to water, and they responded to him fully. He started to think of the land as a big ship. Dirk admired him.

Steve became a Captain in the Police Guard. It consisted of 1000 men in neat uniforms, with rifles and pistols. Its job was to protect the people. All the people were one big family. Many had relatives in the Guard. Trouble came mainly from outsiders in the country.

A few rebels came from Nicaragua to land on the jungle east coast…to cause disruptions wherever opportunity presented. Some of the Guard went down the railroad to deal with them. They had a machine-gun and fired at jungle movement. The Guard backed off.

We had a meeting.

There was one old Thompson with the drum in the stock room. Regarded as a relic, and not in good repair. Dirk told us there was military hardware available at the Antigua black market, and they even had a batch of Al's old drum guns in cosmoline and in top shape. The Guard could do better with them as they came with built-in fear—the bloody Chicago typewriter. It was the Guard's philosophy to deter rather than destroy. But these arms were a water world away.

We came up with a P.R. ploy! It concerned using poor ole Matt Capone. Kill Matt's cover. Down to the jungle. Put bandoliers of 45 slugs across his chest. Put the old Thompson in his hand. Take photos for distribution in Nicaragua to rebel sources. He is running a detachment of the Guard, and takes caught rebels down to the jungle—for a firing squad. No one knows about it up front. Behind the scenes they are calling it "Capone's Jungle Cruise." Many rebels are not fanatical, and they would shy away from adventures in Costa Rica…If the photos get back to Costa Rica or out in world, we say it is just Nicaragua propaganda to discredit the Guard.

Matt did not like it! But finally he agreed…to sort of make amends for the past of the name. It could do good in this case. We had a stop gap. Photos were sent out by devious means.

But it was decided that the Guard would have to get fire power to be used to put out local fires. The machine-guns would only be taken up for these venturings. Planning was started for a future voyage to rectify the situation. The people of Costa Rica did not want to establish an Army. Thus there was no take-over power for any would be dictator to use, nor any excuse for a nearby dictator to attack them.

Ted found swarms of bright children seeking schools. Eager to learn. It was a tradition inherited from the Pioneers. The country was founded on education and the coffee bean. So the program of building schools was beefed up. Coffee profits were diverted to this, and no one objected. The people wanted it so. Ted admired them.

Hydro-electric plants were being constructed. There was plenty of water from the many rivers and streams coursing down from the uplands. Electricity would soon be everywhere.

Two soldier of fortune people, expert jungle killers, were sent by Steve down the railroad to Limon. Their mission was to find and eliminate the rebels on the east coast. The invasive problem required drastic action. They could destroy the railroad.

A training session was set up for a group of 50 men from the Guard. This detachment was to learn Marine Raider tactics. The jungle coast was too vulnerable to invaders from Nicaragua. The detachment would be able to deal with the problem.

The Captain gave talks to gatherings of people on political procedure toward a more real Democracy. They actually amounted to a philosophy of love for mankind. He said the history of Costa Rica had a good start by the Pioneers. He praised the men in the past who had worked to establish a Social Democracy amid the dictatorships. The people were right to desire a free life in a Garden of Eden.

The children flocked around him. "Tell us sea stories." They said. He caught the drama and mystery of the sea in simple language, and wove gentle principles of living into the tales. The schools invited him to visit in all regions. Soon the working people came to hear him.

"This is a great man, and he has no arrogance!" a leader observed. "We should elect him our President."

Captain Lamont became known across Costa Rica as "our papa." He loved the people, and they knew it. Political figures looked at him askance, but no one would offend him. They saw he was just content to be with the people.

Despite the lovely women who flocked around him like the children, he did not take to any one of them. Instead he sent for Tiee to come from Tahiti to Costa Rica. The plane fare was paid for, with the request. She came.

Her beauty and innocence seemed at home in San Jose. But she said right off, "I want to live on the beach, and not wear clothes." She spoke direct like a small child.

"Her words go right to my heart." A young man standing nearby said.

The Captain arranged for Tiee to stay in a hut on Playa Hermosa. It had a thatched roof like that of Juan to the north. There was a vast stretch of gray sand beach in a world of limitless sky, sea, and sand. She lived in it for two weeks, and became lonely.

"Perhaps you would rather live aboard our ship?" Lamont offered.

"Is there swimming?" Tiee asked.

"All you want. The cove is beautiful like you, and remote."

As she came on board, Bert went into happy shock. "You are some sight for a dying old man to see! It has been lonely here. Now our little world has become paradise."

Sporty was almost wagging himself to death. Tiee picked him up in her arms, and he started kissing her bare breasts.

"Sporty is a lucky dog." Bert said.

Tiee put him down, and dove off the stern for a swim. Sporty leaped into the water to swim around with her. Happy creatures in a wonderful world.

While they were eating some fresh fruit on the deck, a group of scarlet macaws flew by screeching. Tiee was back in Tahiti.

Back in San Jose, a student asked the Captain what Tiee could be doing out on the beaches?

"Killing the snake." He replied. This was a well known answer the poor Banana workers gave the angry bosses when they wanted to know what the workers had been doing out of sight. They had been dozing off for a rest under the trees.

Tiee and the Captain were the talk of the plazas. People were eager to know more about them. But they were such polite people, they did more wondering than asking.

Tiee appeared to be a dream within a dream to the Costa Ricans. She was a child of the islands. Tall, tan, and tantalizing. Sweet talking, gracious in manner, with a direct and disarming look, she was captivating to all. The palms, the beaches, the sea, and the sky had their echoes in her.

A wealthy man of San Jose said, "I would give her anything she wants, but she does not want anything." Her desire was in Nature and the Captain.

"How do you like our San Jose?" an official asked her. .

"It's an unhappy happening." she replied, "Too much of things going around not made by God."

"God?" the official said, "Do you know him?"

"I love the Great Spirit, as does my Captain," she said simply, "We walk in His Hand of Love."

"You live in your own world."

"No, in His World."

Out of my deep concern for the Captain I had to ask Tiee some questions.

"Does he ever mention Lenora?" was the main one.

"We have talked a lot about her. You know the Captain is sort of a God among men. She was a Goddess. She was the right one for him. The Evil Power took her from him. He will never put it aside. I am happy to fill some of his lonely place. He loves me too, you know."

"Yes." I said. "Who could not love a creature as lovely as you are, Tiee? He is a sea Captain. What will you do when he goes to sea again?"

"I will go back to Tahiti and wait for him to come and spend his days with me there. He will come to me in time."

"Why not stay here in Costa Rica? We are helping to form its golden time."

"The people are wonderful, but it is too close to the civilization of Man's Misrule. Corruption will come in no matter what you do."

"Tiee, what do you know about Misrule?"

"The Captain told me all about it. I do not like it. Tahiti is more away from it all. We live simple in our islands."

"Bless You, Tiee." I added.

SECRET CONVERSATION: Don Pepe, Dirk Caser, and the Captain.

Don Pepe, the Great Man of Costa Rica, wanted to see our ship. "The Flying Kate" had entered his thinking. He came aboard to the surprise of the crew, who were visiting Bert and Tiee, and Sporty too.

Many were already calling Don Pepe the Father of the country. He was a thin man of high forehead, dark eyebrows and deep eyes, sharp nose, and a wide mouth of thin lips which appeared capable of saying great things. When he saw Tiee, he threw up his hands.

"My dear, you will shock our people. If you come to town, please put on one of our lovely dresses as gaily colored as your inner spirit. What a lovely creature you are! Ah, there is so much contention here these days, I would like to leave for your islands. But I will stay and bear whatever is necessary for the good of our people. We must have Democracy."

Tiee came over and gave him a kiss on the cheek. He was highly pleased. Sporty jumped on him. This pleased him too. He was pleased to meet the crew. He shook Capone's hand, and said the cook was the most important man on any ship. "no." Willy said, "The Captain is." "No." Don Pepe said, "The Captain must eat!" Everyone laughed to see the Great Man arguing with Willy.

"Now we must talk." Don Pepe declared.

The Captain took them below to a table remote from the deck. It was a good private place.

"Like those large granite spheres of stone we have, there is a mystery that bothers me. Some call them the bowling balls of the Gods. Anyway, Dirk, how did you manage to phone San Jose from out here when the phone system does not extend to here as yet?"

"When the refrigeration unit was put in we had a small radio installed as an integral part of it. Due to our running close to coastal waters, the radio could be extremely limited in range and size…a few hundred miles was good enough. You could look at it and not see it…nor could you operate it easily. It is hidden. No one was told about it, except the Captain. It could be used for an emergency. Need to know basis. The crew would not be able to talk about it ashore, nor fool with it aboard ship. It is a rule that whoever uses it must speak as on a phone, and complain that the phone service is lousy. You can use it if something of importance comes up while you are here."

"Our situation in Costa Rica grows ever more serious." Don Pepe revealed. Factions are striving to take power from us. They are of various persuasions at home. We must establish Democracy for the good of our people. Elections must be allowed, and they must be honest ones. We must never join the dictatorships. No individuals must be allowed to abuse our people. The Captain said there are snakes in the Garden and outside the Garden. He is right. That may be the way of the world, but we must not allow it here. People need freedom to live right. The exile Calderon and Somoza have gotten together up in Nicaragua. We can expect an invasion any time within a few years. When they are ready, they will do it. Already some are coming in to do sabotage and spying. I am going to arrange that this ship will get a cargo of coffee to exchange for guns. Sorry to make gun-runners out of you. We need to get military hardware for our Police Guard. You will be making a voyage in the near future, Captain."

"It will be for defense?" Lamont asked.

"Of course." Don Pepe replied. "You would make a good President. The people will elect you if you will run. I would support you like you do me. We love the people."

"I am only a sea Captain." Lamont replied, "My heart is in my ship and in the sea."

"That is sad news for Costa Ricans." Don Pepe said.

The dinner bell sounded on deck. Now Mr. Capone would prevail.

Chapter 9

We were waiting for the coffee harvest to make the coffee voyage to get guns. The berries, called cherries by the workers, were starting to turn toward red...from green to red to ox-blood in color. Then the processing to put the beans into the bags would come. Coffee money would buy the military hardware of the black market. The black government in Antigua had stored up weapons ready for sale in containers that come in off ships. They dealt in special weapons for war use.

Life in the huge bowl containing the Grid of San Jose was varied for us. We went to dances and religious festivals, and bars by the University. Travel was by snaking roads that went up and down amid the saints and shrines of the countryside. Rich volcanic soil. Spring climate. Happy people with dark faces, who think white. The Tico man had a straw hat, moustache, T-shirt, and a happy look...and he was out to do merry-making after a hard day's work. Drinking and dancing were his delight. On Sunday he would go to town, attend Mass, talk, shop, walk around the plaza. At times he would go on a picnic with his colorful ox-cart. People gathered in the parks of towns to flirt while a brass band filled the air with waltzes and marches. Small cafes, called sodas, served the black beans and rice with additions. In San Jose, the National Theater appeared like a palace in a mud hole. Scrap-wood shacks and haphazard metal structures made up shanty towns in nearby suburbs. Prayer meetings took place off dusty streets, near iron-fenced cemeteries and bars. The narrow streets were lined with one and two story wooden houses built flush to each other, and the rain would drum on their rusty roofs. Broken sidewalks and deep potholes caused jokes about natives drowning in them after rains. Small pulperias or general stores offered social havens of billiards, bars, and benches to sit and talk upon. Street vendors with push-carts hawked their wares in the dust. The profusion of people and buildings presented a Babylon of poverty.

We were becoming able to see that Operation Goodheart was just that.

In Escazu, the city of witches nearby, there were the better homes of the wealthy. There were women in the area who cast spells. Iron fences surrounded the homes.

The Captain gave little talks for us. He said he wanted his crew to be in on the Know. He claimed that what you don't know is what finally kills you. It seemed right to us...and we thought it to be the stuff out of which a sea change comes.

"Here the children of the sun and the corn have crept into the white world of the Pioneers. There is mixed blood now. Do you not see how beautiful these people are? They are, you know. They are white with dark faces. All people are of the white light inside. God is the Father of all. So we are all brothers and sisters! The Bible teaches this, and it is always accurate. It is the five deadly passions of the Negative Power that causes the discord. Men love them because they are exciting! But the yogi union with God is the most exciting of all! This means overcoming the passions for your greatest good."

"It seems to me that only saints and rich men have it made." Steve said.

"There are no saints. There are only some men who try to live God's bidding. The rich will do anything—except share their wealth with you. They will only do some benefits. The wealth is what makes them who they are on the earth plane. So they manipulate things to keep their wealth. The regular suffer. Thus the rich grow richer and the poor grow poorer. It has become the ways of this present evil world. Greed is whatever you keep gaining beyond what you really need. What does a man need? It's food, clothing, and shelter. Man should look at things thru the eyes of God. Instead he makes himself blind...and sees only what he wants to see for himself. Money is a good servant, but an evil master. The Dark Power, who is in a battle with God, is always there to stir the passions and blind man."

"You would make an excellent politician for this land." Ted said.

"No, my destiny is elsewhere." The Captain told him.

Ted's wife had died young of a heart attack. He had taken refuge in books. He had developed an immense store of knowledge. He had a small library aboard ship.

"Pass your knowledge on to the children. Give talks. Try to put it into stories. They are so eager to learn. Get your priorities straight. Regroup, reorganize, redo. Make the methods you develop work. The school system is of top importance. We want more teachers than policemen in the country. Tell them that knowledge is necessary to make right decisions. And right decisions are needed for Democracy to survive in the world." The Captain advised.

Willy was harping about visiting the volcanoes. We made a trip out to Volcano Arenal to the north. There was an ominous haze around the cone volcano. Red, yellow, and orange lava was flying up and running down the slopes like snakes from the underworld. Crackings and boomings filled the air. Rocks the size of houses were being blasted one thousand feet into the air above the cone. Smoking cinder-blocks were rolling down the slopes. Willy wanted to go in closer. We did not. The volcano had killed a number of unwary people who climbed close for a better look.

We got Willy away from the fiery shower of the most active volcano to the nearby ones at San Jose, which were approachable. Volcano Irazu presented a moon landscape, gray and desolate amid a huge crater with some smokings. "No fire," Willy objected. Volcano Poas had a vast crater one mile across, with a many colored pit, gurglings, smoking fumaroles, and a greenish sulfur lake at the bottom. A geyser would send a column of gray mud high in the air at times. It was cold at the summit. A rain fell on us, and we took shelter under a plant called poor man's umbrella. The volcanoes were failures. Willy was in love with Arenal.

Wandering about with the 4-wheel vehicle, we saw a profusion of colors in birds, plants, and flowers. Scarlet macaws were obvious beauties. But in the cloud forests the "bongs" of the bellbirds sounded down from the canopy. Great kiskadees sounded their own names. Such birds were more interesting than the screeching macaws. The hot lips flower held up a red mouth to the butterflies and hummingbirds. Electric blue morpho butterflies flashed amazing neon colors. Toucans were in the trees using their huge yellow bills to get seeds. It appeared to be a Garden of Eden created by a happy God. The ten thousand foot backbone of mountains allowed many variations of the plants, flowers, birds, and animals to surround San Jose. There was no poverty in nature here.

We visited some homes in the outlying areas. Some were painted green or blue or pink. That's the way happy people do things. Workers made tiles for roofs by patting soft clay over their thighs. Most houses had grass or palm thatch roofs, dirt floors, no windows. Chickens ran in and out of the house. Outhouses were in the rear. Inside there were religious pictures, family photos, and bright prints on the walls of the parlor or sala. A prominent place was chosen for the school diploma. Poor beds for the kids. Iron stove stood on a wood platform. Firewood was stacked in sheds. Herbs and vegetables were grown near the house. A macaw or parrot or songbird was in a cage hanging on the porch or patio. Tin cans and boxes were hanging down with flowers or ferns. Clothes were washed in a concrete sink. It was primitive, yet functional.

"We need to get them into better houses." Ted observed.

Matt was happy among the people. He would pat the children on the head, and give them fruit or candy. His past had nearly faded away. He was making better responses to Steve's sarcastic comments.

"Go to church on Sunday and murder on Monday. That's O.K., just business" he said to Matt. "Chicago's good name has been ruined by your people. People all over the world know about the Valentine, Cicero, and the Chicago Typewriter." Steve summed up.

"I'm not going to live in the negative past anymore. This is new life for me. I am Matt. The cook, not the crook. I agree with the Captain who said to let the killers remain buried at Mt. Carmel with the bishops."

Peace Corps was printed on our khaki clothes to distinguish us from the Police Guard. It was for our doings and our cover too. This would remain too during voyages and the ports.

The volcano adventure had sparked Willy up. He talked about Arenal like it was a paradise place. He was waiting to go back.

"Fire has such intense color, and it is so alive! It is beautiful!" Willy informed us. "But I would not want it to harm anyone."

Steve was now calling Arenal Willy's woman. He called the volcano Madame Arenal and declared it to be Willy's love in life.

"You like to haunt people." Ted told Steve. "and you are good at getting up their ghosts."

Steve took Willy in hand. He was hoping to scare him silly...which Willy already had more than his share of in life. Willy could talk funny.

The locals told Steve about the black Shaman, who lived in a shack near the edge of town. He had come up from the banana plantations on the jungle coast. They said he could conjure up things. Steve wondered what he could do with Willy.

"Let's go see the willies doctor," he said. "He must be a fire-gazer who could give you some great pointers."

They took a local with them to translate findings. The Shaman made some incantations while he brushed Willy down with a green branch. Then he threw a handful of explosive powder on the fire. Willy was happy.

"Agh, Agh," the Shaman exclaimed, and he put his hands over his eyes. Then he started to rattle off a lot of talk.

"He sees fire coming down by your friend." the local explained.

"Better stay away from the volcanoes," Steve advised Willy, "Do not visit Cartago. An eruption there killed people in town. Arenal is off limits for you, Willy."

Steve danced around and gave his reaction. "Who do the voodoo. He do the voodoo. Woo. Woo." The Shaman got up and danced too. He was happy with Steve.

Many weeks had gone by. The National Liberation Party sent word from the Legislative Center that they were pleased with our efforts. The school system showed the most advances toward a Democratic reality. The children were like a sponge in absorbing all the facts and knowledge that was manifested. Teachers were thrilled. Health conditions had improved in San Jose and across the country into remote regions. Soon electricity would be available everywhere. Housing was slow, but construction was on the increase. The economy was moving ahead and starting to improve the life of all.

Then the word went out. The bushes had turned red, and the beans were ripe and ready for the picking. Swarms of pickers went into the dusty fields. They had on heavy shirts and wrappings around their legs and wore rubber boots. The ox-blood berries were picked into baskets, and these were dumped into carts. There were mills to scrape off the hulls. Slime covered the beans, and this was soaked away. The beans were spread out on concrete platforms so the sun could dry them. Finally the skin remaining on the beans was rubbed off. They were then sorted and polished. The beans were stored in rough bags. The gold of Costa Rica was ready for export.

Sarchi ox-carts were used to transport the bags of beans to the port of Puntarenas. Long lines of the gaily colored carts made the eight day journey downhill. It looked like a festival procession. The wheels were a cross between the Aztec disk and the Spanish wheel, with very intricate designs of gay colors. The five foot high wheels were squeaky, had their own individual song or chime due to a metal ring striking the hubnut, and were hand painted with pointed stars and lovely flowers. The drivers said it was sad the oxen did not have the capacity to appreciate such beauty. But one driver said: "You never know." The oxen would just plod on down the road, which was more a trail.

The ship had to be brought down the Gulf of Nicoya to the rickety dock at Puntarenas for loading. Chinese dock workers took the bags off the carts and carried them into the hold of the ship. They received pay from Dirk, who treated them well. Soon the ship was fragrant with cargo.

Sporty went wild. He started sniffing the bags, and running around the decks in a frenzy.

"He is not a coffee drinker." The Captain commented.

Back in town, Matt was happy. He had discovered the chimi churri sauce made with coriander.

"This will make grilled meats taste like they came from the kitchens for the Gods!" Matt said to me.

"Where is that?" I asked.

"How the hell should I know?" he replied.

Willy was having his black beans and rice, plus fried plantains in a soda. At a table next to him in the café was a rather repulsive looking tourist from the U.S.. Most likely from a backwater in the swamp country or industrial area. He engaged Willy in conversation.

"You all from the U.S.?" he started.

"Yeah," Willy responded, "But I have been working here for quite awhile."

"Ah, conning the locals in some way. That's the way to do it. You all get what you be able."

"No," Willy objected, "I'm helping out."

"Doing the sec stuff, I betcha."

Steve came in the door. "This guy bothering you, Willy?"

"Ah sure would like to bother Willy." The man said.

Steve came toward him.

"Back off afore ah flings a snot on ya!" the man threatened, his finger up his nose.

He never had time for what the kids call a bugger. Steve floored him.

"Let's get out of here!" Willy wailed. "The Police will come."

"I am the Police." Steve said.

Steve and I were opposite buddies in the hometown...grew up together, fought gangs back to back. He had a mean mother. I blamed her for things. I could tell you some nasty things Steve did, but won't. May forget sometime, and do it anyhow. Hope not. Anyway, we fought together in the rotten fruit wars. There was this gang across the tracks in the far part of town, and they would come in on us at times to beat hell out of us. It had twins in it that were mean guys. They were the leaders. One time they were up on top of the A&P building in winter waiting for us. A frozen grapefruit came down and hit Steve in the head. He went down and stayed there for half an hour. When he awoke he became raving mad, and was going to go to their area and finish them off. We had to hold him back until he cooled down some. Only the unknowing and the unwise trifle with Steve. I am the only person he never hurt in the hometown. That is, those who came into his life back there. He took care of some very mean guys too. The town seems so remote now.

"Steve should have been with you in the Big War," Ted said.

"I often wished he was at my back in that Green Hell they call Guadalcanal, Ted. He is a good guy to have with you in nasty times. Instead he went to Europe ran across the Remagen Bridge under fire. A sniper put one through his stomach and elbow. He fell down, rolled over, and got one off that took the sniper in the throat. That German fell out of the second floor window dead. Steve's arm shrank small and white. The docs wanted to cut it off. He put it in a sling, hauled it around, and forced it to comeback by his mind. Steve is a hard man. He knows I understand him. I think he might have some love for me after all we have been thru. I have never spoken against him. He married an English girl during the war. She was attractive and intelligent. I visited them often where they lived near Oak Lawn. One night he offered to share her with me. She was willing."

"No thanks, Steve, I can't abide adultery." I answered. "The Bible is a book of Wisdom."

All was ready to go to sea. The Captain was eager to sail out upon the deep. His ship, waiting now at the dock in Puntarenas, would become again a living and organic creature of the sea. Others took up our endeavors, and we left San Jose. It was exciting!

Amid the excitement we found Bert dead in his bunk. He had told us he wanted to be buried in the white earth of Cabo Blanco rather than the sea…up on the white cliffs overlooking the sea at the bottom of the Nicoya Peninsula. This old sea dog had helped us a lot, and we would honor his final desire.

Tiee said a tearful goodbye to the Captain. She kissed Sporty too, and cried over Bert. She would go to San Jose to leave for Tahiti. The Captain rightly told her the voyage would be too dangerous for her to come along.

She stood at the end of our wake waving to us, until the distance took her and only the wake of the ship was to be seen.

Off Cabo Blanco the Captain sent the hook down to hold on the bottom. We put dear old Bert in the small boat, and took him ashore. It was a hard climb up to the cliffs. The white earth was soft and we went deep down. The Captain did not make a speech. He said: "Bless you Bert, go and be with the angels." We knew he knew the Bible, and that the dead go to sleep in the grave until the Resurrection comes unto the Judgment. We understood he was saying that Bert had been an angel for us. At rare time the Captain could be devious in his thinking. It was sort of like his expert conning of his ship through a maze of islands. Amen.

It was more than a three hundred mile run to Panama and the Canal. More near four hundred miles with a lot of peninsulas to our port side. The ship kept fifty miles out to sea to clear the Peninsula De Osa, where Drake had landed to tilt his ship up on the beach to scrape its bottom for better running. Right past it we came in close to the Peninsula De Burica. It is a long finger of land jutting out into the sea, strangely divided between Costa Rica and Panama right down its middle. We ran along the coast of Panama past an island and a huge Peninsula and turned hard to port to come up to Panama and the Canal.

The Canal was like running down a river and then crossing a lake. It took time, and Sporty was on deck voicing his disapproval of it all. He did not like strangers confining his ship and fooling with it.

Out in the Caribbean Sea the Captain put the helm hard to port again, and we headed for the port of New Orleans. They were paying the highest prices for coffee at this location. Days at sea took us there.

We had a lineup muster each day for inspection. Then an exercise routine followed. We joked that the muster was for the Captain to tell Matt to change his dirty T-shirt. The military routine gave the crew a strength and a pride. Our Captain knew what he was doing. He was kind, gentle, and loving. Could any crew ask for more? Matt took care of the inner man too. Our adventure made us want to go out on deck, look at the shining sea, and shout in the sunlight.

The River was dirty. The port was a highly complicated maze, and deep within a strange city. We were happy to get good money, turn, and run the delta to the open sea. Now came many more days to pass Puerto Rico and Cuba and run the islands to the large island of Antigua.

Sporty kept us amused with his antics. He was such a happy dog. He loved us all. I thought his diet of fruits, vegetables, and grains (same as ours) was doing it. At times we had some fish. Matt made everything taste so great! No need for meat.

Antigua is famous for English harbor and Nelson's Dockyard. The Admiral had anchored his fleet there. It is run by a black government. We were to see a Mr. Duval. We saw the containers lined up, some of which held military hardware.

"Welcome, Captain Lamont." Mr. Duval said, "We have heard much about you. The grapevine, you know. It is true you have a real Capone with you?"

"Show him your family photo." Dirk said to Matt.

"This is wonderful! We do not usually get such distinguished visitors." Duval admitted, "We can supply your needs. Captain you have a movie ship? It is certainly a strange ship. We have not seen one like it. Do you have movie women aboard? We would welcome them ashore to wine and dine with us."

"No women." Lamont replied, "We have an exciting dog you should meet."

"Captain, I don't think we are talking about the same thing." Duval said with a funny look on his dark face.

"Well, down to business, gentlemen. We admire Costa Rica. We are a dictatorship here, but sort of in between the governments if you know what I mean. We will give you a discount on the weapons you require. A little help, you know. We need to be kind and help the children. We make money here to help our children too."

"What is available?" Dirk asked.

"The latest! We can provide two rapid-fire cannon, a flame thrower, a few 50 calibers, and plenty of hand machine-guns. Some grenades too, if you want them. And plenty of ammunition for all too."

"What, no atomic bombs?" Steve quipped.

"Surely you are joking, Mr. Steve?" Duval said.

"No, Willy wants one. He loves fire!" Steve said.

"Mr. Capone, we are going to make a gift to you of some old drum guns like your famous brother had in Chicago. They are left overs from the era, which were passed on to us. Everyone wants the military clip type these days. Your Guard will appear much more frightening with them. Better to scare away enemies than to shoot them, perhaps? There are only nine. Can we have a photo of you holding one?"

Capone sighed. "If mama knew about this! Al would have loved it! I'm only a cook!"

"What is he saying?" Duval asked.

"It's just his lament." Ted said.

"Where do you voyage to now?" Duval wondered.

"We are headed around the shoulder of South America, and down the continent to go around the Horn." The Captain said easy.

Duval raised his eyes to heaven and crossed himself. "Heaven forbid! Don't do it! A number of brave sailors have died in the storms and are there now down in those wild waters forever. The Atlantic and Pacific Oceans come together there and do battle at the Horn. It's the no man's land of the waters! Anyway, your cargo will make excellent ballast."

"Sort of like Guadalcanal." I commented. "The Jap and U.S. forces came together, and many brave men never left that stinking island."

"Man is fragile. He should avoid all forces." Duval insisted. "Don't go there. Watch yourself south of here too. I'm sure there has been a spy of your ship. Your cargo is worth more than gold to those who kill and rob. Do not let any boat approach you. Boats have been found destroyed, and people dead or missing near here. Drugs, you know."

"O.K." Steve said, "Have your men mount one of the cannon up on the wheelhouse. Will the roof take it?"

"This new cannon has little recoil. The roof can handle it fine." Duval said proudly. You can engage a boat at a fairly long distance too. The explosive shells are deadly. You will have to be careful you do not shoot away your masts. By the way, what does that Peace Corps labeling on your uniforms mean?"

"It originated in C.I.A. thinking." Dirk explained, "We are the forerunners, the harbinger, of what is to come in perhaps the next decade. You know, like John the Baptist. Young people of the U.S. will have jobs to go out and dig wells, help build churches and schools, teach better farming methods, improve the economy of countries that need help. All to establish peace in the world. We are doing this in Costa Rica now."

"Will you be able to give us some help too?" Duval hoped.

"Of course." Dirk answered.

Dirk gave us a party at the top tourist restaurant of English Bay.

The Captain spoke up. "The Horn is the greatest adventure of a lifetime. Many would do it, but do not. They fear it. Rightly so. Extremely dangerous because of the williwaws and great storms, cold, and desolation. Perverse currents and howling winds. The supreme test of a Captain, his ship, and his crew. Anyone who does not wish to go can leave the ship and fly across to Costa Rica and wait for us there. You wanted adventure, we will have it."

"I am with you Captain." I said, "You can do it!" The rest of the crew agreed.

We headed south, striking off to the southeast, to round the shoulder of the vast continent full of amazing contrasts of dense green jungles, great snowy mountains, hot dry deserts, and huge cities. The fabled city of Rio de Janeiro was our destination.

Duval's warning came to pass right off. A fast boat of size was under our plume of black smoke off the stern. Steve took the cover off the cannon, worked the loading mechanism, and set the sights for the distance. It roared out fire, and the shells flew all over the roof of the wheel-house and rattled down to the decks. Sporty ran for his dog-house.

Behind us white splashes rose in the air around the pursuing boat…and it took off at right angles in another direction. It was lucky to make it, and probably suffered some damage.

"They cleaned the cosmoline off a Thompson too for us…said to give it to Mr. Capone. For use up close, they said." Steve informed us. "I'll do the gunning!"

"We want to tilt the Law of Karma in our favor by shooting not at, but near to them. Those who show mercy will be given mercy. Only in direct defense will you fire directly." The Captain instructed Steve.

Chapter 10

A storm at sea, some distance to starboard, dropped its dark curtain of rain down to the surface of the sea. We were running again in the realm of the circular vastnesses of the surging sea and the phantasmagoria of the sky. Our ship was a speck of wood with living entities existing in its limiting confines, moving on the surface of a watery world. Days at sea become different only in color movement. The mystery and beauty of that world disappears in the fading light of the sea sunsets. Night brings the starry deeps of space—as the Great Jeweler casts His diamonds across the dark velvet cloth of the night. Then is it any wonder that the Captain and his crew would pray on the deck each night? Love does strange and wonderful things to the human mind. Our Captain would watch us with a look that had no earthly origin. We were a strange ship in a violent world.

Just before the end of the day, the sky cleared of clouds and the sun shone briefly upon the waters. The sea spread subdued on all sides of the ship. A flaming sunset, behind billowy clouds on the far horizon, shot great rays of red into the limitless dome overhead. Twilight came. The after-glow of the sunset burned, slow and steady orange faintly fading, in the arc of space above darkened sea horizons.

The night was intensely beautiful. Sea glow sparkled in the swishing wash of the "Flying Kate's" bow and flickered in the myriad fires within the wake behind the stern. Countless stars filled the vault of space. The mystery of universes upon universes glowed in the starry heavens above us. Meteors flashed down in the darkness over the sea. A majestic moon, full and free, rode the night skies. It silvered the sea surface.

Matt lay drunk on the stern under the splendor of the starry sky. The photo at Antigua had been bothering him, and he had found Steve's hidden bottle. He took to bellowing, raucous:

"Oh, the dirty Marines ate all the beans,
And shit all over the submarines
Hinky Dinky parlay Vooooooooooooo……"

Matt rose to his feet, and babbled wildly at the stars above. The bottle flew from his hand and the sound of the breaking bottle went forward. Being too unsteady, he dropped back down and went to sleep.

Steve came upon him. "Disgusting, really disgusting!" Steve exclaimed. He picked him up and took Matt down to his bunk below.

"No more nips, no more nips, he killed it off." Steve mumbled to himself.

Steve took an oily rag, went up on the wheelhouse roof, and took to wiping down the cannon and its shells. Salt spray was in the air at times. Then he adjusted the waterproof cover carefully over the gun, and tied it down well. The security of the ship had to be protected from the sea. He did not like the idea of passage around the Horn.

Daylight dawned upon a sea of peace and beauty. The waters pulsed, in great swells, like the systole and diastole of a huge heart. The ship was running smooth on the sea.

In the wheelhouse the Captain put Willy on the helm, and then he went on deck to sit down and relax in the beauty of the bright day. All was very well. Sporty jumped up in the Captain's lap for some petting. Matt came up on deck bleary-eyed. The Captain smiled at him. He turned away. Steve said nothing.

"Till the war-drums throb'd no longer, and
the battle-flags were furl'd.
In the Parliament of man, the Federation
Of the world." Ted mused.

"It's a good day for such thoughts," the Captain told Ted, "Tenneyson had his dreams for mankind. But we must be accurate in wisdom. The Bible says wars and rumors of wars. We will find it so. Yet it is our task to work for Peace. Blessings come to the peace-makers. But today we can experience a bit of perfection. The glory of this day is ours! Look at the sparkling sea around us! We are in the lap of the Father, just like Sporty here!"

The day dawned, steely gray, with a slow rain falling. Everywhere the watery wastes washed in peaked whiteness. Three points off the starboard bow a ship was plunging like a whale gone mad. High overhead a bird, fork-tailed, wheeled in the sky, sharp eyes on the wakes of the ships.

The bow of the "Flying Kate" cut well into the surging waters, and the Captain increased the speed and veered off to port. Ginger tea kept the upper part of us secure, and the pounding of the sea was only felt in the feet. Soon the other ship was distant on the sea.

We had become seasoned seamen. The distances at sea are vast and it takes interminable days of incessant sea motion to cover them. Our routine proved to be a solid base for us...and the Command Confidence of the Captain developed in his crew too. We could do anything on the sea. Yes, a strange ship and a strange crew, indeed! The Sea Wind had blown us into something rich and strange—a Sea Change!

Both the prevailing wind and the current were against us in this region. The Captain slowed the ship to save fuel. Dirk was happy about that. We had extra capacity for our long runs.

At night, on the approach to Rio, the Southern Cross appeared in the sky. The Captain did not consider it to be an accident in the heavens. Steve had a somewhat different regard for the constellation.

"That is what comes from Matt destroying my bottle." Steve said.

Matt looked sheepish. "I should have kept it for cooking." He reflected.

"The glory of those stars will be welcome for our night prayers to keep this ship from all harm," Lamont said, "It is the symbol of the Ages." Many sea weary Marines had taken strength from it while in harm's way.

"We can stop at Rio and take a walk on those mosaic sidewalks. We will find an anchorage at some out-of-the-way dock. There is always one somewhere in a big city." The Captain informed us.

After the days at sea, the massive coast of Brazil came up like a dark cloud on the horizon to starboard.

We encountered the Doldrums. Our ship had entered a belt of equatorial calm. The orb of the sun burned down on a glassy sea. The ship's screw churned still waters, silent, oppressive, without wind. Heat rose from the decks. It shimmered above them, like the heat mirage on highways in mid summer. Sporty sought the shadows. We rigged a canvas. Got under it, and Matt brought us iced ginger ales. Nothing moved on the sea. Not even a huge turtle rose up from the deep. Life retreated from the surface of the sea. Torpor.

"It's going to be extremely cold at the Horn." The Captain said, mopping his brow.

We ran in close to the shoulder as it came up starboard. We headed down to Rio. It was a city to see.

A search around found the dock we were looking for away from the tourists. Matt decided to stay aboard ship on the watch. He did not like restaurants much, and was happy where he could do the cooking. Definitely not the tourist type.

We took off walking inland, found a bus, and rode for Copacabana Beach. The vast crescent of the good time charlies was booming and loaded with girls, and guys trying to score. Seemed sort of a hippie heaven of sand and water.

"Look at those girls!" Steve said, "They have hardly anything on."

"I prefer beautiful women," Lamont replied. "The girls can't get up to the Seventh Heaven.

"Where is that?" Willy asked, "At the end of the color sidewalk so wavy and promising something?"

"It's where sex ends and turns to love." Lamont revealed. "It's Heavenly!"

"That statue of Christ on the mountain seems to say O.K. to all this scene, with those arms wide open." Ted said.

"Not likely. He would not approve. Much is going on here. His followers are few." Lamont answered. "The little world of our ship is far better."

Back at the ship Sporty suddenly came alert. He was hearing something. Matt took up the Thompson, and looked out on the dock. An armed gang of young men was getting out of a van. Matt stepped out and caught them with their guns down.

"I'm Matt Capone, brother of Al, and I'll give you a Valentine like his if you do not get the hell out of here! I'll make you and your van into swiss cheese!"

They looked at the drum of death—and they left with the wheels smoking.

Sporty came on deck. "Damn good decision!" he told Sporty. "And you really are a C.I.A. watch dog." Matt was shaking.

We returned to the "Flying Kate" to get the outgoing tide at dusk.

"Give Sporty some of your ice cream." The Captain said to Matt.

Steve said he would have turned the cannon loose on those bums. He said they were out to rob up some dope money.

"What in the city?" Ted questioned. "Are you insane?"

The lights of Rio faded in the velvet of the tropical night. There was the scent of green land on the slight off-shore breeze. Sporty put his nose up in the air. The night became deeply dark, and the far off glories of God appeared in arc of space. The sea below washed in phosphorescent fire. The Captain called for prayer.

We voted to leave the modern monster of concrete and confusion that is Sao Paulo alone. The captain set the ship directly down for the Falkland Islands to save distance. Dirk approved. He acted like he was on vacation. Sporty sniffed his leg. "Don't you pee on me!" Dirk said.

"A horny dog is a healthy dog." Steve said. "He was most likely thinking of doing a hump."

"O.K., cut it!" the Captain ordered.

Matt was our hero. He tried to act like Al. We all laughed. Told him he was a lousy gangster. Definitely not Al.

"Well, those punks in the van thought I was a gangster!" Matt said.

"No, it was the old Chicago typewriter that scared them off!" Steve insisted. "Duval was right."

Drizzling at daybreak. The overcast had become a leaden sky, without wind, weeping upon a subdued sea. The ship moved in the half light of a damp and dewy world. Life on the rolling deep became listless. Sporty went into his house, and stayed there. There was a subtle change toward cooling in the air. Extremely wet world.

The next day was dark, cloudy, and wind. The clouds were lead cotton. A stiff wind whipped the surface of the sea into large waves. The ship pitched and rolled through rough seas. It's prow plunged into dark waves, vividly blue, topped with white crests. Relentless motion. Our bunks became desirable to escape much of the motion. We started to call Willy "submarine." He was under the covers most of the time.

There was now a chill in the air. We had purchased cold weather gear in the U.S. for use at the Horn. Out came the sweaters and woolen hats. We had a sweater for Sporty, and he was happy to let us put it on him. We did not yet know what cold is. The Horn was going to be a hard teacher.

Finally the Falkland Islands appeared dead ahead. We were in cold and stormy seas. The fearsome Cape Horn was just to starboard and a little south.

"Actually three oceans come together down here to create whirlpools, perverse currents, icy waters, and terrible storms." The Captain let us know. The air was freezing cold already. The waves were higher and wilder. "The Antarctic Ocean sweeps in from the west to hit into the Pacific and Atlantic Oceans. It's not a place for frail human beings!"

"Like us!" Willy wailed.

Chapter 11

The Captain conned the "Flying Kate" into the bottle-neck harbor of Stanley. We received a warm welcome. The weather was already running bad with high winds and sleeting. The people in the Falklands took it in stride. They invited us to tea and a hot meal.

We set about preparing the ship for stormy and violent seas ahead. Hatches were batten down. Portholes were covered. A hose was run over the ship searching for leaks. Those found were either stuffed with rags, or filled with the building foam. We would be dry and warm below. Sporty would leave his deck house and sleep with us. There would be waves sweeping over the decks at times. Extra anchors were purchased, and also hundreds of feet of holding line.

At night the White Arch could be seen in the blackness over the region of the Horn. The west wind had brought in storms upon the swirling seas there. The sky Arch is the terror of seamen. The Captain only smiled at it. He had confidence in his ship.

Our course was set for the Estrecho de la Maire, the Strait off Cabo San Diego at the end of Tierra del Fuego. Named after a brave man. It is here the vast water forces of the Oceans meet in a fury of currents and storms. Highly hazardous to all ships. It is the no man's land of the watery world. At the rocky tip of the continent of South America.

The yellow oilskins with hoods protected us from the horizontal spray, but it had sleet mixed in it and the bits cut our exposed faces. A frosty snow-ice formed on the ship. Sporty lifted his tropical feet in amazement at the cold. Then he took to eating the snow crustings.

"He thinks it's Matt's ice cream!" Ted yelled.

Williwaws suddenly struck down off the rocky uplands...gusts of wind roaring out to sea at Hurricane speed. (Force 15,100 knots) They caused hail-storms, coming from drastic changes in the weather.

We were almost knocked down. Sporty ran down below yelping.

"He thinks the Gods are throwing stones at him!" Ted exclaimed.

Sporty had looked at the surging sea—and he was scared. We had looked at the wild waters---and we were scared. Our trust was in our

Captain who was not scared. The ship was creaking, and groaning like the wind. The sea and wind groaned like a huge sick giant turned to water. The Captain did not express any fear—he was happy at the helm. His ship responded well to his touch, even tho the poundings below made our ankles feel like a heavy chain was on them.

An albatross landed bold on the bow, after the gusts had passed on to sea. Oh, that yellow eye looking over that yellow bill! It was hard and cold in its stare. The bird was a large mess of feathers on the rail. Willy was close to him at the railing.

"Look at that wingspan! It has to be thirteen feet!" Steve yelled in the wind.

The wild bird let our a startling scream. Willy jumped, and would have gone overboard into the icy waters except for the safety rope.

"Damit! That is scary!" Ted yelled. "There has to be the soul of a dead seaman in that bird!"

The black-browed bird spread its large wings and wheeled around to the stern and took to skimming the ship's wake.

"Matt had better throw more food scraps out so that awful bird will leave us alone." Willy advised.

We were running out now in the Pacific. The Isla Hornos was below us in a group of small rocky islands. The moaning of the wind increased to a roar, and became a scream when it reached our plunging ship. The millibars of the barometer went from 997 to 984 to 979 and down. We were in Force 15, 100 knots, steady blowing now...hurricane winds. The cross seas heaped up into mountains of swirling water, and the wind was tearing the tops off the giant waves. The "Flying Kate" was rising high and then going down into the valleys like a surfboard.

A greybeard, coming across thousands of miles of ocean, and building four times higher than the huge waves, picked the ship up...and coming down its terrible slope, the ship went over on its side. The icy waters came aboard. We were hanging by our ropes! It seemed the end. No ship had ever been able to come back up from a capsize.

The Captain, waist deep in water, concentrated through the wooden hull to the stern. The propeller was out of the water. So too the rudder! We were helpless! No control! He held the wheel lightly—and suddenly threw the motor wide open! For a few seconds the screw had slipped into the water as the ship was sliding down the slope! It bit into the water and the ship lurched ahead to come back up pouring water. We were back up and heading down the valley! We all raised our hands in salute to the great sea Captain who could read the ship and the sea. Our lives had been saved in seconds no other captain could have fathomed. He had kept his promise to keep us out of the deep.

"God Bless you, my men." Was all the Captain said to us. He had saved us at the Horn where many had died. This was something that not one of us would ever forget. Something that other seamen would not believe.

Sporty was unhappy about it all, very unhappy. He kept close to us after this.

Instead of going down around the Cabo de Hornos, the five by two mile gray rock hump that is the Horn, we turned to starboard to run the Canal Beagle to Puerto Williams. There we would anchor, rest, and fuel. Chile had a Naval Station there, and the people were known to be friendly to ships that dared to run the Horn.

The waves were long and gray now, with black clouds overhead. Cape pigeons, pintado petrels, small brown birds with white checkered mantles, were following our ship. They were skimming the waters behind us. We had queasy stomachs, and Matt had thrown food overboard. Our ordeal was the good luck of the wild birds. Eating is prime in the wilds.

South America is a huge heart of land full of amazing contrasts. It has great mountains, jungle, large cities, and some dangerous men out to rob and kill in remote places. Pirates and bandits. The bottom is a drowned mountain range—a bewildering maze of waterways and barren rock swept by cold winds. Near the tip are glaciers coming down to the sea. The ship becomes a floating speck on the immense waters. Our voyage around the continent was a long one.

Above us an immense glacier loomed. A long stream of icy water came out of its snout to run into the Beagle Canal. We moved in for a closer look.

Sporty ran to the rail. He started growling at the glacier. Being a tropical dog he did not approve of it. It was something that should not be. We were all laughing.

"He must think it's some kind of a monster worm. This place is making our happy dog unhappy." Willy observed.

"After getting hit in the ass with ice stones and then being rolled over, he must think something is after him," Steve said, "And this must be it!"

"The glacier is groaning and making grinding noises," Ted said, "He thinks it is trying to scare him."

The weather cleared. Puerto Williams stretched out before us at the foot of the wild mountains. Its line of gaily-colored houses was dominated by a large church. Simple rectangle clapboards, yellow and white, with peaked red roofs, gave shelter from the harsh climate. Below was the line of docks. A radio tower rose up on the right. A Navy ship was tied up at the docks. We tied up right next to it.

The friendly Chilean people were curious. They invited us home for a hot meal and tea.

"Where did you voyage from? What sort of a ship is that?" Where are you going? Did you have a hard time in the storm?"

We let Dirk make up the lies. He is a most devious person, and surely must have studied the art of lying? He gave them the proper picture for the situation.

"The storm hit us hard and rolled us over." Willy blurted out.

"You mean it heeled you over some." A naval officer corrected.

"No, over!" Willy insisted.

"Not possible."

"We have the greatest sea Captain there is!" Willy answered.

The Captain laughed. "It was some storm out there." He said.

"Are you thinking of making a movie out here?" the officer inquired.

The C.I.A. takes refuge in being vague. "It's a prime place out here for an adventure movie." Dirk told him. He had a "movie company" contact the Base way before we arrived. The prospect of dollars upon dollars for the locals blinded the Base. Special treatment. We suspected Dirk of doing this all along our route. He pulls the puppet strings behind the scenes. We should know.

There is a mountain saddle of land that curves down behind the Port. The jagged summits of snowy peaks that stab the sky are behind it. We went for a hike over the saddle.

The view was astounding! A mountain to the left rose up higher than the others. We felt sure no one had ever stood on its snowy summit. Nor had man trod upon the snowy slopes out here. Pristine! A wilderness of rock and snow! We wondered about animals in it? Too harsh?

The higher scene was lost to Sporty. He was happy running around and peeing on the land. It would belong to him from now on. "Just look at him go!" Willy said.

Bright sun weather is brief in this region. The mountain snow glares in the hard light. At dawn and dusk the low light gives a pale red or deep purple to the snow, the clouds, and the granite summits. Our 7 x 50 binoculars, night glasses, gave great views in the lesser light.

We stayed in town until the black clouds started to stream in and lay low upon the land. Snow was in the offing. Soon the blue waters would become a steely gray. Icy winds would whip down on the town. Time to hunker down in the woolens and oilskins. Those on land would retreat into the buildings.

Tierra del Fuego has no fire—it is an island of barren desolation, gray granite stone, snowy peaks, glaciers, low clouds, wild winds, primeval, remote. It is split between Chile and Argentina. Only a few hardy people inhabit it. It is the wild tip of the heart. The gray rocky land at the water is cold and harsh in desolation. There are vast stretches of stormy sea.

We decided to travel the Canal Beagle in a westering direction going north. The open Pacific is a thundering water giant here smashing on the rocky edge of the continent. The inland passage through the maze of waterways would be good for a thousand miles. We came to a place where the Canal opened up into a huge lake. Down anchor for the night. Set long lines on the anchor to avoid dragging. Keep away from tangling kelp beds. The winds were up in the howling forties region. Sporty got up on the Captain's bunk to snug up and sleep with him. He felt safe with the top man.

At dawn a williwaw hit us as we got under way. Sheets of spray flew over us with the sound of shrieking sirens. The prow of our ship kept cutting thru the waves. The variations of gray rock and sea water were unbelievable. The Captain conned the ship through the maze to the Strait of Magellan.

Punta Arenas was up the way. It is considered a center of civilization in this remote land. But it is a backwater place like the one in Costa Rica. Punta Arenas is a poor port in a remote region. In earlier days Black Pedro had done his massacres here. We had enough of Punta Arenas's. We headed west down the Strait toward the Ocean, into a hard blowing wind.

At Isla Desolacion the waters started to broaden out. It had Cabo Pilar at the west end, known for heavy rains and waves over the deck. It stuck out in the Pacific. We could hear the thunder of the giant breaking waves on the rocky shore. The vibrations reached our ship thru water and air. We made a sharp turn into Canal Smyth.

Slowly we were coming up out of the bewildering array of watery places and changes of weather so overwhelming to a ship. The Great Ocean slamming down upon the rocky shore of a Great Continent creates forces that belittle and confuse man. In the immensity of waters, rocks, clouds, plus winds, the ship was like a chip in washing machine. In the lulls of the storms the condors and vultures were ever wheeling on the wind, seeking the remains of non-survivors below. When they came low white patches appeared on the wings and neck of the black vultures and their wings made whistling sounds in the dismal air.

We were still battling weather off the Pacific. The dark masses of rocky land, patched with snow, along the watery passages, were ever under the lowering black clouds. Sleet storms came in gusts off the heights striking the ship and moving rapidly on. The northwest wind brought howling storms from the pacific. The "Flying Kate" kept cutting into them with its strong prow. Our black plume and white wake were marking our route around the huge continent. During brief breaks in the weather there were boiling masses of cloud to starboard, and above them the glare of the sun reflected off snowy peaks. Other times heavy rain poured down on the ship. All was steely gray. We moved on for many miles.

The land turned green with small trees, and bushes coming down to the water's edge. Here and there, we spotted hardy Indians gathering wood to pile up by their wooden houses that seemed to be always falling into ruin. These simple souls were boondockers who rejected the centers of civilization to live lone. They stared at our ship in wonder.

At Puerto Charrau we anchored near green trees. A four hundred foot waterfall was thundering down into the trees. "The sound of descending water in the wilderness is spiritual." Our Captain said, most happy with our anchorage. We agreed. Stay forever! Dirk said never on this. I think the Captain was with us.

"What would a modern man do without a library?" Ted had to say.

"And hep women!" Steve added.

"Fire?" Willy asked. "No fire engines and sirens?"

Matt said nothing. He had thrown up his hands at the Horn region, and was morose about things from then on. "This foul place has ruined my meal-making! Get the hell out of here fast!"

Dirk did say we could take our time in returning to Costa Rica. He had called from the Chile Naval Base to what we now referred to as our tropical paradise. In the cold darknesses, we had forgot about the wiles of man back there, and the other snakes too. "All is quiet in Costa Rica right now." he informed us. We thought Dirk would like a vacation rather than a voyage. The Captain started thinking......

Nearing Puerto Eden, we saw piles of shellfish marking the sites of long gone Indian living places. Millions of mussels are available for the digging on out tides. They are seven inches across. Today, everyone's food!

At Puerto Eden, Steve talked with a tall Indian who called himself Bart. He was scary looking. A shock of dark hair overhung his scowling face. He had hard lips and haunted eyes. A broad nose separated the two. It was a hard time face. It was the old story of encroaching civilization ruining a simple way of life, and pushing the Indian into a background of poverty. It was obvious he did not like newcomers to his scene.

"Give me some shirts." he demanded.

"The Captain gathered up some spare clothing, and gave it to him. "Bless you brother," he said to him, "Go and raise up some fine children in peace. Indians are good. Love the land, and love others."

Our ship continued northering. The Captain conned it across the huge bays and thru the channels between green-gray masses of ever rocky land. The whiteness of the lone Andes Range was ever starboard. The whiteness of the winter peaks across blue waters.

The brown and white petrels and the black-browed albatrosses had been with us for much of the voyage since the Horn region. We called the latter "Willy's Scare Bird." The petrels were small neat little birds. Matt would feed them off the stern at times…..like someone doing bird-feeding in his backyard. He never tried to feed the jumping porpoises. He was a bird man, not a fish man.

"I have always wanted to fly in the air." he revealed to us.

"Matt, you are not an angel!" Steve reminded him. "You are headed for Mt. Carmel in time, you know. Bad company there."

"Don't be cruel." Willy said.

Our inland passage, just less violent then the open sea, would come to an end up ahead. There are fifty miles of open sea across the Golfo de Penas, and ninety more yet to Bahia Anna Pink for inland running. The Gulf is known for violent storms and perverse currents where the Pacific Sea slams inland.

"It's a prick of a place." Steve warned us.

The inland passage was not an easy place of going either. We had seen the wrecks of large ships all along the waterways. We were fortunate in having a Command Captain like no other ship ever did have. He could read the waters in whatever form or way like a book. Sporty was tuned in, and he knew the Captain.

Sporty had strange experiences on the voyage. At the Horn he got scared and stayed at our feet. He got peed on that way. Finally we got wise and sat down like a woman. Steve told Matt he was an old lady anyway.

There was the blackness of storm at the Gulf. Huge swells came in from the Ocean. Heaving seas and howling winds filled the Gulf. We were in the heavy stuff again.

"It's harness and ginger tea time again folks," I said, "One for the shoulder and one for the belly. Let's do it!"

Sporty did not like it. He knew the harness meant trouble. But being a trusting dog he let us strap him up. He licked the Captain's hand.

We headed into the darkness of driving rain and waves washing against us from the north, with long swells moving under the ship. The crossing of the Gulf was a time of moving in all directions. Sporty took to the relative stability of his deck house, but a wave came on board and that drove him back out to the wheelhouse. There was no need to haul up a bucket of water to flush the scuppers at the stern. They had constantly running water.

After the hard won crossing the ship still had plenty of open sea to run around Cape Raper. A long stormy run finally got us to Bahia Anna Pink where a large ship named Anna had found a safe anchorage in the mists of time past. Here we sailed back into the inland waters.

Now we had a long run through a huge maze of drowned sea-islands. At their end was another Gulf to cross. We were seeing more people right along now. Halfway we anchored at Puerto Aquirre.

Those who gave up being lone boonies gathered up into sort of a town here. Yet it was still wild country. This was the last gasp of civilization before the desolation to the south on the way to the Horn. Punta Arenas? We considered that place the behind hole of the continent, and the same goes for it in Costa Rica. Strong prejudice on that name. Forlorn places and odd shabby people.

We stayed over a day amid the clapboard wooden buildings and dirt streets. Beached on the shore were canoelike boats full of crossbars to hold them together. Water travel was the only way to get around here. It was oars and sails. No motors. Children played among the boats. They gathered around the Captain and he told them stories.

"Story telling seems to be your profession, Captain." Dirk said. "When we get to Puerto Montt, you will be in your glory. There you will have plenty of people as well as children. When you dress up, you really become an imposing sight! Speaking does it too! My tired mind will take a vacation there. Right at the end of Chile's railroad and roads. Sort of civilized and sort of wild too. Most important there is clean air, clean water, clean food, and clean people. We could regain our health here, so to speak. All is relative, you know. I hate the toxins of civilization. Am willing to accept the overcast in the climate."

"Wow!" Willy commented, "That is the longest speech you ever made!"

"I feel like letting my hair down. But secrets are off limits. We can talk about the foolish things like ordinary people do. The other things must remain in the dark to save their ass. The deep dark knowings belong only to the C.I.A."

The people were full of questions about the ship and us.

"We come from nowhere, and we are going nowhere." Dirk told them. "This is the movie ship of the movie 'Harpoon.' Did you see it? We are thinking of making another out this way."

"I want to be a star." A dried up old fisherman called Fishbait admitted. "The sea is in me from many long years on it. I can really act up after some drinks."

"I'll sign you up." Matt said, coming up with a little notebook.

"Do you know who this guy is?" Steve asked the old man. "He is Al Capone's brother!"

"Who is Al Capone?" Fishbait inquired.

Matt gave him a hug.

The Boca del Guafo was a short run. The island Guafo was in the Pacific at the entrance to the Gulf. It split up the swells coming in from the long haul across the vast sea. The large peopled Isla of Chiloe was off our port side. Gulfs were everywhere. So too were small boats carrying market vegetables and sheep. Our course was up the extensive Golfo Corcovado to Golfo Ancud and the Puerto Montt just beyond on the mainland of Chile.

Running the east shore of the large island, we met dark-hulled boats sailing to the market in Puerto Montt. They were loaded to the brim with sacks of potatoes and vegetables fresh from the earth, lumber, sheep, homemade items, and the man's hard-working wife and yelling kids. Most of the small boats had the gaff rig that raised its high peak to the wind, and the oars would be brought out when the wind would cease. There was the smell of tar as the hulls were preserved with the pitch. Each boat had its blend of smells.

Churches were in many places up on the island of green rolling hills. We heard the bell, and anchored below. Climbing up we visited the locals in a church. We explained that we were seeking Dirk's vacation place—away from the wind, the weather, and the sea. They at once suggested Castro ahead of us...up at the end of a narrow arm of water.

"That's the place you are looking for!" an old man directed. He seemed to be wise in the ways of Chiloe. "Puerto Montt is too busy." He warned.

After a good run, past many small boats heading for Puerto Montt, we went through a maze of little islands and found the narrow arm of water. It went up deep into the huge island. The land closed in on both sides of us. Eight boats came in with us loaded with barter and people.

There was an open market along the waterfront. Its stalls were full of fresh vegetables and sea foods. Around the small settlement were fields of wheat, and potatoes, and cattle. The town had a hotel, a church, and warehouses, and small wooden buildings. The people had dark hair, Indian faces, and looked like they were standing in the shade. They were friendly and open to us—and curious! The docks were loaded with sacks of potatoes.

"Rural commerce here." Ted said, "Rather nice to see."

We anchored to stay awhile. The ship appeared spectacular in the close quarters of the small harbor inland. We became the talk of the town. The word went out to Puerto Montt too. Steve had told the girls we were a movie ship scouting the area out.

"Stop spoofing the girls and trying to do sex." The Captain warned Steve. "These girls have some wild brothers. Don't create a hornet's nest here for us."

The Captain found an attractive widow. She had a small seafood restaurant going. Her husband had drowned out there in the Great Sea, and left her with a brood of kids. They swarmed all over the Captain like bees on honey. She had a small house near town, with no rooms in it. Lamont stayed with her in the house. It was cold, so a blanket was used at night. One little boy tried to raise the blanket. Life was basic on the Isla Chiloe.

"Our Captain is a Honey," Willy said, "And he makes the widow be the Queen Bee."

"He is the dream man of all lonely widows in the world. It is sad he can only grace the life of so few. He more than fills the void, and gives them new life and hope." Ted said.

Ted took to teaching in the local schoolhouse. The people honored him with fresh produce, which he brought to Matt on the ship. The young regarded him a hero who had gone around the Horn. They always asked for a "sea lesson."

Willy was wary of the girls. He was uneasy around the older ones. But he found one who was a chain-smoker of cigarettes—and he was happy to watch her do the tiny fires all day long. It fitted in easy as many of the people were heavy smokers.

Steve had a sexy girl. They would go cavorting into the fields of wheat that ran up and down the nearby hills. He lived like a bull in the pasture.

Except for the Captain, we all had the ship for our hotel. We had to keep cautioning Willy not to let his girl burn the ship up. Smokers are not compatible with a wooden ship.

"Hang out on the docks." Ted suggested.

"Myself, I spent time writing notes, and petting Sporty. And, at times, exploring the bucolic countryside. Most of the time the sky was overcast with clouds. But this made the colors of the countryside more interesting.

Weeks went by and became months. Dirk was happy to have it so. He took time off from his manipulations of people and events. "Just floating along like those clouds up there." he told us.

There was a great thing happening in all this screwing off. Matt took over the kitchen of the widow's seafood restaurant. It soon doubled in size. Her children became well dressed and looked more healthy. He beamed when we mentioned it to him. He trained the widow into becoming a special cook.

"Matt will leave some good behind him." The Captain said.

"It looks like upper New York around here, and with the cool climate too." Ted said in praise of our refuge. "Only the overcast is too much. We are still on the edge of the stormy region of Chile."

Then Dirk came out with it. "It's time to move on." he said simply. "We can go up the bay and take a look at Puerto Montt before our turn out to the open sea. It's a lively place to be."

The Port at the top of the bays is the focal point for the commerce of the Southern Region. Trains and buses moved, blowing out black smoke. There were cargo and naval ships tied up at docks. Buildings and warehouses were larger. Osorno volcano loomed up. The mountains were brilliant white with snowy tops. Angelmo harbor was full of the small sailboats lying on their sides, and being unloaded into carts drawn by horses. They were plain work carts, unlike those in far off Costa Rica. Various industries, businesses, and shipyards were in operation. Tenglo island protected the mouth of the Harbor. Powerful sea smells rose from the busy stalls of the seafood market at Angelmo. Vendors, hefty and talkative, sold abalone, mussels, silver mackerel, shrimp, and various fish. The seafood was either fried or made into soups and chowders. Here was the port at the end of the world. It was the ending for Chile's railroad and roads. The flow of goods went both down and up. For the little sailboats of the huge island it was a magnet. The busy Port had high-pitched roofs, fancy balconies, and seafood restaurants. Even wood stoves for sale to the country people.

"Millions of mussels for food. Women working happy. Men talking all day. Children playing. This is civilization. The modern world beyond has toxic money wheels and deadly wars. It is not civilized! Here it is the Simple Love living." The Captain commented as our ship finally entered Chacao channel to get to the open sea.

The twenty-two mile waterway had shallow places and rocks. Our Captain conned the ship easily through the dangers. We were still wearing our woolen sweaters and hats just like the people back in Castro. At the port of Ancud area we made a starboard turn, went past the mouth of a large river, and made for Valdivia. Green trees yet, but soon the long desert coast of Chile would be off our starboard for many miles. We could feel the Pacific swell moving under the ship.

Chapter 12

We were running fast now due to the Humbolt Current and the Southeast Trades being with us going north. But a heavy storm came out of the west, and we found protection behind a headland until it blew out.

Valdivia was the City of the Rivers. Three came together there, and it was located on one of them. It had good beaches and ancient Spanish forts. We spent a day exploring, and then took to the sea.

Coquimbo was interesting in that a Norway ship had wrecked here in the early 1900's. Its load of pine lumber helped build some of the present structures. Its bell was up in the tower of a local church.

The desert coast of Chile was a sharp contrast from the snowy mountain maze below. The rugged Andes Range was now a backdrop to desert beaches and low coastal mountains. It was more remote and desolate—and a dangerous shore should a gale send the ship upon it. Our lives depended upon the motor running.

We decided to make an excursion to Machu Piccu near Lima. Matt organized a picnic for us in the mountains. Local buses banged along dusty roads to the area.

"These people were lucky the Spanish soldiers did not find this area. They were rapacious. History seems to prove man is an irrational animal living in the mode of ignorance. Gold is a poor goal to have. But man loves the deadly passion of greed." The Captain said, looking at the ruins before us. "The saving Holy Spirit is available only if you seek it."

Sporty had his idea of the ruins too. He peed on them.

"Look at that!" Steve said, "He does not think much of what has been done here."

"Man's misrule is cruel. They liked to cut human hearts out," Ted said, "And the bandits around this area will still do the same today…but with guns. It's not religious anymore, but just greed."

Willy looked around. "Let's get out of here!" he said.

Almost to Ecuador, we came to Punta Aguja, and saw Sechura Bay around the bend. It looked like an excellent anchorage for the night. The

Captain took the ship in, and dropped the hook near the shore. The weather was calm. We could have a good night's rest from the sea.

Just before daybreak, Sporty gave a growl. Steve leaped up in bare feet and got to the cannon. He saw the dark hulk of a ship blocking the way to the sea.

A shell screamed past our masts and hit the beach. Another came tearing thru the corner of Matt's galley. It holed the superstructure and screamed on.

The rattling roar of our cannon filled the bay. Steve raked the ship along its waterline. The bright flashes of the exploding shells showed in the dark hulk. Pieces of bodies and metal rose in the air, and fell to the water. The ship disappeared in the water. There was no one swimming on the surface.

"Damn!" Steve exclaimed, "That's the end of Black Pedro and his crew!"

"It's more like Black Juan up this way." Ted said. "Bandits who left the horses for a pirate life. Kill first, then rob. Thanks for saving us, Steve."

"The authorities will not know about this. They will not be missed anywhere." Steve said.

"Did they know about our cargo, and seek it? Or was this a random attack by self-styled pirates from Peru? Or was this a try by the Dark Forces to prevent the defense of Costa Rica?" the Captain pondered.

"If they were seeking our cargo, they would not fire on a ship carrying ammo. This could blow the cargo away. It was not a knowing attack." Dirk reasoned.

"The Negative Power would want to blow up the ship and cargo. As of right now we carry the defense of Costa Rica in our hold. This Evil Power that dominates the earth plane could invoke negative men to do what would appear to be a random attack. There is more than meets the eye in the events among men and nations." Lamont answered.

"Costa Rica is like a small sheep among wild wolves. It is striving for Democracy amid a passel of dictatorships. It can make it only with our help." Dirk added.

We left the coast of South America, and headed directly out to sea in a beeline for Costa Rica. It was a long sea distance back to the tiny nation around the vast continent. Now we had only a few days of sparkling sea to run.

We came around the Peninsula De Burica, and were off the coast of Costa Rica once again. Our ship sailed into the Golf Dulce (Sweet Gulf) to anchor for the night. The hook was dropped near Puerto Jimenez at a remote beach. Jungled hills rose from the beach.

We went ashore for a swim.

The Captain seemed heavily preoccupied. "We should revisit here later on," he said to me, "It's a peaceful place."

We ran up the coast to the port of Puntarenas. The cargo was unloaded, and taken up to San Jose. The ship would remain to operate as a patrol vessel from this base.

Dirk decided that the second cannon should be installed on the "Flying Kate." Costa Rica now had a navy! Rebels would no longer be able to come down in small boats at night and land on the shores to sneak inland to join groups at San Jose.

There were a lot more coastlines to watch over on the Pacific side. Landings on the Caribbean coast were easier for rebels, but then they had the difficult jungle to traverse inland. Coming down from the northern border they were quickly detected. The Pacific coast had their attention.

Once supplies were put aboard, we went out on patrol. We found an inlet an Nacascolo in the more remote Guanacaste region. This allowed the ship to operate in the Golfo de Papagayo and stop all boats trying to run the shoreline.

Right off we encountered three small boats from Nicaragua in the night.

"Turn around, and get the hell back to your border!" Steve ordered. He fired the new cannon and threw water all over the boats. They went back up the coast fast as possible.

Word spread about the terrible ship. Soon patrols were not needed. The "Flying Kate" had helped the cause of Freedom again. But in other parts of the world, young girls were waiting for "the movie ship" to return. Steve was all for going back to some of the ports. He had sex memories.

The Captain ran patrols for a few months, and then anchored the ship in the hidden inlet near the top of the Nicoya Gulf. He loved the

"Flying Kate," and hated to leave it to continue working programs in San Jose.

Dirk put Juan aboard as a watchman, and he was happy with small payments that seemed large to him. Dirk said he was a bargain.

Dirk told Juan he was now a captain in Costa Rica's Navy. If there would be future patrols he would go along. We even got him a khaki uniform of the "Peace Corps." Because there was pride in having no Army in Costa Rica, we dared not advertise a Navy. So now the ever-changing ship became a Peace Corps ship. Juan was a very peaceable person. The workings of the C.I.A. are as strange as they are mysterious.

Strange things were always working out in Dirk's balding head. It was amazing how he had conned us hometown boys, and the Captain, into his scheming. His unlimited funds put the clincher on it all. Money makes the merry-go-around go around. (no, it's not really the motor that does it) And, in our case, he used the flag too. He had been trained in the devious ways.

We had captured a few rebels out on patrol. Steve was threatening to shoot them, and he was a convincing guy when it came to violence. Dirk questioned them. They told him about the rebel camps across the border in Costa Rica. Near the Rio San Juan. At the end of the dirt road from Pital. This was the most remote and uninhabited territory in Costa Rica. After a rain the road became a quagmire that stopped vehicles.

Dirk wanted to investigate those camps. We took off in our vehicle for Pital. It was indeed the end of nowhere. The dirt trail ran out of sight for twenty-five miles. We hoped for no rain, and ran the road.

Sporty did not like the bouncing ride. He is a smart dog. The seas, the volcanoes, the glaciers, and the violent people, are all monsters to him. He was willing to do without them in his happy living. To prove it he always had his peer ready for action.

Willy was happy carrying his flame-thrower. At Antigua, he had been shown how to carry it, and how turn it on and off. No proper training at all. But he had seen the fire, and that was good enough for him. It was wonder to have and to hold.

We heard voices ahead. Coming around a curve we saw three men standing in the road. We got out. Dirk yelled out something in Spanish. They responded. They were wondering who we were? Since various factions were involved in the intrigues, it was difficult to know who was talking to whom.

Willy was scared. Men with guns! His finger was shaking on the trigger.

One of them shifted his weapon. The flame-thrower went off, and the deadly fire arched over on the three men. They ran screaming and dying in the road. A horrible sight! Willy sat down in the road and wept. He refused to touch the flamer.

Steve picked it up with the intention of putting it in the store-room of the Guardia Civil. It was the most nasty weapon in the military realm. He knew it would be needed in time. The tiny nation was bound to be imposed upon. The Guard would finally grow into an Army, and the coastlines would soon demand a Navy. Steve knew this to be the way of the world.

Back in San Jose, Willy left the room when someone would light up a cigarette. He could not abide fire in any form. He suffered a sea change. He put his energy into organizing fire brigades in the rural areas to protect the people. He taught the children to go to streams and rivers with buckets, made available for fire water. He became a fire chief in the city. His desire for fire was finished.

Dirk and the Captain were invited to a secret meeting in the offices of the Legislative Assembly. The Captain insisted I be allowed to accompany him. The meeting was not to form any policy, but to compare notes and to speak generalizations pertaining to Costa Rica. Seeking new and special insights.

It was agreed that the social reforms were forming up rather well. They held great promise for the future. Rural people were being brought into the picture more. Less poor. The rivers were being exploited to provide electrification out to the remote areas....but the cost was hurting the economy....too expensive! Schools showed the most improvement. Health was now better, and housing was more available. The economy was going up and down with the coffee market. Bananas were highly helpful. But diversification was needed. Dirk presented his viewpoint, and the Captain voiced his wisdom.

They asked me to say something. Most likely, out of curiosity.

"Being a Guadalcanal Marine and a hard-bitten newspaper man, you can't expect me to say nice things. Such sayings are balloons that burst quickly anyway. Hard thinking will help to preserve your paradise....your tiny nation full of good things.

A large increase in population is coming due to your paradisiacal aspect and relatively toxic free environment. This will compound your problems across the board.

Right now you have sort of a comparative golden age. Your decisions toward money can make it burst like a soap bubble. Strike a balance if you can. I, for one, would not like to see smog forming in this beautiful valley. Have mercy on the children, the birds, and the flowers....on all living things! And yourselves, of course.

Modernizations will bring their corruptions. Yes, look at the mighty U.S.!

I see a projection of the deadly passions of anger, lust, greed, attachment to material things, and vanity. Anger brings wars, and murders, and a specter that is haunting the world even now! Lust creates overpopulation. Overpopulation is the root of all problems. Or it is money? They might be interchangeable. They create each other. The deadly duo! Greed overrides human rights and values. Material things tend to destroy the spiritual in man. Vanity causes all the preceding passions. Take a look at the old kings in history. Your challenge is not to follow them. I see that you are trying to do right here---and it is admirable!

I want to present a wisdom saying to you. It will not be noticed right now, for its time has not yet come. But it will be more than noticed in a few decades! Then it will go around the earth worldwide—and many will use it, even in commercials! Terrorism is in the wings! It will not pass you by. I will put this saying out on the wind in the last decade before the year 2000.

ANYTHING CAN HAPPEN TO ANYONE ANYWHERE AT ANYTIME.

This is the darker side of things. If you want the positive side you can get if from Captain Allan Lamont. Note that he is loved by children and dogs. You can't snow the troops or newspapermen. Nor can you fool the kids or animals. And he is highly intelligent! Here is a great man who would make a great President! One I would vote for."

There was some hand clapping.

The Captain was happy with my small speech. He told the legislators he did not desire to be a President.

Dirk and Steve pondered the security of the little land between two continents and two oceans. They agreed it was in a precarious position.

"Leftist groups were working within like termites, but the free elections kept defeating them. The people kept voting for Freedom, even tho establishing social reforms right along. Freedom was always foremost in their minds. Our Government will spend money on peace rather than war. The primary way to defend ourselves is by Education. We will be the Good Guy living on the land in the Garden of Eden. Our social groups will work together as brothers. We will hold on to our good Colonial start as small farmers. We have come through and off the base of coups, revolutions, revolts, and dictatorships—to a hard won Democracy. Here we will stay! Our national hero was a farmer. Our school children do the parades on Independence Day instead of soldiers. We are inclined to be non-violent. We have no death penalty. Those early explorers called us the Rich Coast, thinking to find gold here. Instead we are a Treasure Place of birds, flowers, animals, and friendly folk. Our riches also include good climate and good government. Brothers in a Democracy! All this spells Costa Rica!" Don Pepe said.

"You did spill some blood." Steve replied.

"Only to survive. It was sad for us to do this," Don Pepe said, "and now we are starting a National Park System to help the land survive too. We hope to preserve at least one third of the beauty in our nation."

"There is an insidious enemy within your borders in the mountain wilds off Panama," Dirk informed him. "Your people are great for cigarettes. A Drug Lord is working to switch them to the cannabis sativa, and even the hard stuff. The people are vulnerable to this situation. He has a regular fortress built up down there."

"You can help us with this problem?" Don Pepe inquired.

"It would take the Army which you do not have to solve it. He knew you do not have one, so he established a stronghold that requires an Army to approach it." Dirk revealed. "We would have to train up a special force to get in there. Even then there would have to be a special method too."

"Do it! Protect our people." Don Pepe ordered.

Dirk made Steve the captain of the venture. He started to take certain men from the Guardia Civil to form a Special Forces Group. One hundred men were selected, and given training like that of the Marine Raiders of War II. In quick, do the job, get out. Shoot first, and shoot straight. Surprise was basic, so there would be little time for a response to the attack.

Night vision glasses were yet experimental, but would be used in a dark attack. It would be done in a hurricane. Ammo would be loaded in pockets so men could stand in the winds blowing hard. Pistols with silencers would be used. Small plastic charges would blow open doors. The men would depend on being expert marksmen…it only takes one bullet. Rain and darkness would put the defenders at ease.

Finally a hurricane came in off the Pacific to sweep over the small nation.

Amid the howling winds in the dark night, the Group got to the house undetected. A few men blew open the doors, and others rushed in. Lights were shot out. A few of the drug people came out of rooms with machine-guns in hand. They were shot dead in their tracks. Others ran around in confusion. Those who had guns were shot.

Steve and his men went into the building until they found the Drug King. He was executed at once. His men surrendered.

"Go back to Panama, and stay there!" Steve ordered. "Return and die!"

"You did a good job." Dirk told Steve. "You saved a lot of lives by it."

"If the first drug dealer to stand up in the U.S. had received this treatment, the U.S. would not be in the shape it is today." Steve said.

We went to the Central Market for the sights, the sounds, and fresh foods. Matt put on a colored shirt, and being in a festive mood acquired a handful of flowers to carry around. He bought a variety of herbs for his cookings. Fresh vegetables and fruits went into his bag. We would be eating good the next few days. He would whip it all up into original tasty dishes. Even Sporty gobbled up his creations.

The Captain was invited to lunch by a few legislators. They were curious about his ideas regarding society and civilization. He met them to the sound of marimba music at the outdoor dining area before the yellow elegance of the Gran Hotel, next to the National Theatre. This superb setting was conducive to Alpha thinking.

"Perhaps you wish to preserve all this?" he questioned, waving his arm around, "It will soon perish in smog and the march of progress. You are at a developmental stage right now where you can still influence your direction of doing." Lamont knew it was a spot dear to their hearts. He gave them a stimuli in a challenge.

"We intend to keep this area for the tourists." One of them replied.

"You should not allow visitors to stay on. The land will attract people coming to live here....in time an inundation. Limit your population too. You have a small country. Run a tight ship. This is a general first principle to follow." Lamont advised.

"It is difficult to keep women from having babies." another said.

"Yes," the Captain said, "You are battling the deadly passions when you govern. See the money wheels going around in the large nations. No one can stop them. They break people, harm their health, corrupt them. It's the modern phenomena! Countless human beings have been done in by them—one way or another. My point is that you are small enough to perhaps control them and go another way. Agrarian would be best for you. You already have the basis here."

"World markets demand that we make and sell products." The legislator said.

"This will bring you all the ills of modern society. It is not the way to go."

"What then?"

"Get off the greed principle. Go stand before a mirror. Look at yourself. What do you really need? Food, clothing, shelter, a motor schooter for transportation, a small electric stove, and a washing machine. Perhaps a few small cars for the elderly and ill? This is a broad base. Details can be worked out. Keep it simple. Avoid complications. Why do this? To avoid the many destructive results you see in society today. The easy way is really the hard way. By proper procedure you can gain the goal. It is Simple Living and High Thinking! All should be directed to this result. Remember that Capitalism creates and fosters the deadly passions. No money wheels! The goal is a Garden! Everyone loves a garden at heart. The world has run on the principle of 'kill you for a buck.' It's Satanic! Do not follow the large nations of the world. I'm advancing you better ideas to work on. Think! You can even install organic toilets good for the land. There are many positive options to explore. Negation does not have to win in the world. If you seek anything more than the basics it becomes greed...more than you need. Remember that this comes at too high a cost. And remember tourists O.K., but no stays."

"Well, you do love the people. But how can you make the basics work?" one of the lawmakers challenged the Captain.

"Each person would work two months on the farm, two months in textile factories, two months in construction, two months in transportation, two months in stove and wash machine production, and would have two months for himself. Thus he would create his own needs. No exceptions, except for the ill or the elderly. Bible says man must work. The worst sin, to the man on the street, is 'kill for a buck.' The wicked work harder to reach Hell than the righteous do to reach Heaven. We need to reverse some things."

"Thank you for saving our cargo at the Horn, but it was not necessary to make a story about it."

"Well, there are too many stories out about rounding the Horn." The Captain admitted. "More important is the penetration of your coastlines. If you will send me young alert men I will train them to form a Navy of patrol boats. I'm sure that Dirk can arrange for boats to come from the U.S. for this purpose. It will be a secret venture, of course."

Ted and I were in a discussion at the University concerning the future of Costa Rica. We were wondering just where our efforts would lead in time. Only the people themselves could inhibit the lasting effects of the movements being set into motion. That was our conclusion.

The local newspaper people came in upon us to interview me about the Captain's feat at the Horn. It had caught the people's imagination, and the newsmen wanted to determine if it was indeed true. They were willing to have me tell them about it because I was a newsman myself. Accuracy is a habit in the brotherhood.

"Explain it to us." They asked of me.

"First, the Captain does not lie, nor does his crew. The Captain is not even interested in having this event told. Willy let it out all over. The Captain saved our lives in accord with his promise to us….to take us on an adventure and keep us alive during it."

"Just what did happen down there?"

"You should have the Captain describe fully to you what a Greybeard is. It is a wave that comes across the sea for thousands of miles and builds up four times higher than the regular huge waves at the Horn. It lifts your ship up to the sky and drops it down. It has done many a seaman in, or is it down? It can pitch-pole a ship end over end for a sure ending in the deeps of the sea. In our case it rolled us over. We were hanging in our safety ropes in the water….and up on the side of the awful wave near the top. It sure seemed the end. The Captain was half under water in the wheelhouse, but as usual, full of his Command Confidence. He is a Master of ships and of the sea. Unlike any other captain, he feels through the ship to the sea below. There was a split second or two when the prop got back into the water, and he opened our powerful motor up full when it did. He bit into that wave and brought the ship back upright! So we went down into the valley and back up on to a regular huge wave. That was it."

"No ship has ever come back up from being over. So it was a miracle?" a reporter asked.

"It is the Captain who is a miracle." I informed him.

Then, as reporters usually do, the reporter moved the challenge to a new area. "You say you are peace corps people, but you run guns and put cannon on your ship?"

"It's just plain necessary to defend yourself, and we do it for the people of Costa Rica too. You can be the Good Guy in the world, and defend yourself so you can be. You have to continue to exist to be the Good Guy. We work for peace."

"Tell us about your exploits and functions on behalf of Costa Rica. What have you done, and what will you be doing and how?"

"Secret."

"The peace corps is secret?"

"Yes, we like it so. We have no interest in any praise for our helping a tiny nation stay on the path to Democracy."

"Then you are political?"

"Not so. We are lovers of freedom."

"That is commendable. We are happy you are here. People here insist on staying free. We even limit our President to one term."

"We know all about you. That's why we are here."

"We will limit our reporting to the amazing feat done by your Captain. It is the stuff that good new stories are made of. Do you wish to say anything more about the Captain?"

"The genius seamanship of our amazing sea Captain saved our lives under impossible conditions. There is not another like him. We love him, and he loves his crew."

GONE WITH THE WIND

Chapter 13

Rebel activity was starting to build up near the northern border….more and more. It was causing Steve to press the Guardia toward becoming more aggressive in actions. An invasion seemed to be building like a dark cloud on the horizon. Samoa wanted to return and run the country that had exiled him. More men were added to the Guardia.

Steve had developed some ideas to eliminate criminals and rebels. They were the same to him. He regarded his actions as fire barriers, burning out places, to stop the big fire from reaching the people. It appeared right and logical to him to take negative action to stop negative action.

"The tax-payers of the nations are carrying a heavy burden of criminals. Jails have become too expensive. Something needs to be done about this. I propose we utilize the volcanoes here. Let the nations empty their jails. Bring the prisoners here. Put a road up to the volcano, and a place to push them in. Truckloads can be done at a time. We can do it for $100 per head. That would be a saving of thousand upon thousands per prisoner. Think of how much money there would be to educate the ignorant, and help the needy! Stop the criminals from harming the people. Be cruel to be kind. We could try a pilot program here first. I am willing to be the devil pushing the deserving into the fiery pit." Steve said at a University talk-out.

"That's wild!" Willy exclaimed.

"But the growing condition of the world says it has become necessary." Steve answered.

"The Tico is a happy-go-lucky guy with a coffee cup in one hand and a banana in the other. No way can you do such elimination in his country. His economy has no room for your proposed venture into the

Devil's business." The Captain told Steve. "You have been walking on the edge of the Dark Side for some time. Now you are going across it. The crew and myself have been hoping to see you learn and lean toward the Positive. You do have a policeman's mentality. Don't you know that they are negative servants? Try to turn your mode toward the Positive Polarity that will finally resolve the earth plane battle. You need to strive to be a winner."

Steve did not reply.

The Captain was storyteller to the children, teacher to the adults, and a fabulous sea captain to adventurers. At the University he gave small talks to students in the fields of religion, history, and philosophy. His talks were of such import as to fit into various other subjects too. A universal wisdom came through them. Same as his refusal to be President, he declined the offer to be a professor in the University. He was hearing a special drummer.

There was one legislator who had become his sounding board in the Assembly. The others always paid heed to his words. The Captain provided enhancement for their deep thinking in a striving to make Costa Rica special among governments.

"TECHNOLOGY IS NOT GOOD FOR YOU! It will undo all the positive movements you have instituted in your society. It should be used only in limited form. A refrigerator is nice to have in life. Do not manufacture chemicals or plastics. They become killers. Beware of the developers. Limit the production of cars. Limit the production of people. Why? Look at the great U.S.

I see a web of suburbs going out from San Jose, and a web of roads covering the country out to the remote regions. You will kill the wonderful one room schoolhouses and loosen the people's ties to the wonderful land. Would you kill the pioneer spirit in the remote regions too? Destroy the forests of the black howler monkeys….and you will no longer hear their great cries at dawn and dusk. You are more danger to them than the harpy eagles that swoop down to get a few. The scarlet macaws will no longer make their colorful group flights so noisy in the air. Unique birds and animals grace your land. Let them live too. Keep life simple and make it fairly comfortable, not complex and overdeveloped in the name of money. Limit your material wants.

Choose only basics. The worst evil giants are within. Greed is one of them. Tech is killing the world.

You converted a fortress into a National Museum. You used coffee to build a National Theatre. You have wisdom. Use it well. Tone down social programs into basic needs only. More is never better. Some is good. Always simplify. Prevent complexities that create complexities. Never compound problems. You have done well—but you are in the danger zone now. The dream of Paradise can turn into a foul stinking bridge between the continents loaded with too many people. All your good intentions and doings can finally disappear—be gone with the wind."

"I fear the Captain is rather right," the legislator said, "We need to think harder and better."

"Never think you are fighting just an organization or political group in forming the future of the land here. You are doing battle with your own deadly passions within yourself. And the Dark Power works thru them. Be aware of what is behind the scenes. Seek the Positive Polarity. What? Of course, I am speaking of God. It is you who are the battleground in the Great Controversy between the Cosmic Powers.

Governments try to solve the problems and fail. Why? Dark forces rule the earth plane in this present evil world. Build a huge church or government and they are taken over. Avoid Global Government. Do not let the ways of the world destroy your vision of a Paradise here. You are small enough to control happenings. We can only find our true destiny in the Great Spirit. A great society must be a spiritual one. The Bible has the Great Design Plan of God in it."

"What Plan is that?" the legislator asked. "I have not heard of it among the governments."

"It is the OverRule of the negative forces. What will finally be. The Coming Kingdom of joyous life in a perfect world. It is sort of hidden in the Scriptures. Only for those who seek to know." The Captain revealed. "Eden restored!"

"Sounds unworldly."

"It is so for now. Only the relatively few followers of the Master of Life and Death, who have escaped the corrupting wiles of the Dark Power down History, live in harmony with it today. The Bible reveals it to be the Remnant Church. The one that obeys the Law and the Testimony."

"There are many churches in man's history. They all do good." The legislator said.

"Study history. There is no hope in History. It becomes only a record of Man's Misrule. The churches teach fables and cater to man's vanity and ego. They do not really teach the Grand Design Plan of the Bible. They do not even know it. Only fables. Man loves fables, just like his deadly passions. He is on a rip-roaring living plunge toward the Second Death! No hope! Then where? The Bible. It is the only book that is one third prophecy that comes true right on time down History. You always get an instruction manual with a product. God gives one with his creation too. If you go against the manual your product does not last long. Is there a God? The universe runs as watch. There has to be watchmaker. Is there a Devil? A corrupter? Look at the wars, the hospitals, the morgues, the crime, etc. on the earth plane. The many churches are negative servants; like the police, they help inhibit destruction only."

"Then which church?"

"Compare each one to the Bible. You will find it."

"Right now we need a plan for Costa Rica."

"Social democracy becomes too expensive. Go back to a rural democracy. Live simple in a complex world. No one can corrupt a man of few wants. He becomes his own captain."

"Each Tico here thinks he is his own man. He guards his freedom well. We in the Legislative Assembly try to obey his needs and wants. He is lax on religion as it is so dictatorial. He sees the dictators and wants no part of their world."

"Excellent! He still has a chance to find out what is really what in life as it is. The religion in the churches can be highly deceptive in practice. Power for control, and money to gain by it is the game. It's an old history story. The pioneer spirit serves him well yet. But freedom is the opportunity to find out the Truth of things on the earth plane. It is a plane of illusions, you know. Your Tico is natural man who can't understand the spiritual, except he become spiritual man. Only spiritual man can understand the spiritual world. The physical is only a basis. He need to move forward and up. Your government tries to allow this to happen in time."

"You could give a few talks, and see what happens. Perhaps some insights would come of it? The University is here for it. You have only presented some hints here and there, and have provoked some thinking. The people like you. They regard you as a great man."

"Seeking is practical. It can solve your pressing problems to develop a good and lasting nation. The Ten Point Divine law of the Coming Kingdom should be followed right now for its top results in society. No one can come up with anything better. Try it, and see. There is a negative side to the Divine Plan. Break that Law and it breaks you. The way of the world leads to the slippery slopes of sin, which go down into the pit of the Second Death. It is imperative that all avoid this ending. II Timothy 2:15 is the key to the Kingdom. Study the Scriptures! All the negation put into the world by the corrupting power of the Dark Power must be eliminated so as not to be disruptive in the Positive Kingdom."

"You appear to be an excellent preacher too."

"Not a preacher, a teacher. My teaching is scientific too. It bears up. Prove your Position. The many others spouting off can't do it. They present fables to the people. There is no power in them. Your task is to find out what really works and find ways to apply it. I seek to reflect some thought to help you catch a vision. Make a practical application of it. Avoid having Costa Rica go down the drain of history as most nations finally do."

"Well, that's a noble aspiration. I will think on it, and pass on what I can." The legislator told the Captain.

The Captain's thoughts, both small and large, had an influence on those who heard them here and there along the way of his life. His crew especially found him to be a rich and strange sea change on the Dark Ocean of the earth plane.

We were having the national dish Gallo Pinto, black beans and spiced rice, plus eggs and fried plantains, at a restaurant near the University, in the San Pedro suburb.

"Hey, we are in San Pedro again, and were in Punta Arenas again at the Horn. What is happening?" Willy observed, "Strange stuff!"

"The gods are shifting us from point to point." Ted said, "Who knows what destinies are determined for men? We go where the wind blows. Every man is a dreamer—even those who say they are not. My wife died of a heart attack, and I turned to books, yet here I am."

"Happy to have you, Ted." The Captain said.

"If my head was split open, hundreds of tiny cunts would come out and run all over the place!" Steve said. "I have never been deep in anything, except what they call sin."

"For the sake of mankind wear a helmet." I told him. "There are too many roaches running around the world now."

Suddenly we heard gunfire!!!

A plane came streaking by, low to the ground, going down the valley. It had struck San Jose. It banked over on a wing and headed back up north to the border.

"Damn!" Dirk exclaimed leaping up, "The dangerous duo are invading!"

The Rebel forces of Somosa and Caldron came out of the camps, and moved down to Quesada, northwest of San Jose.

Dirk, the fixer, who got Captain's papers and port clearances for Lamont, now had an invasion to fix. The Guardia, and a host of volunteers, were unable to hold the military forces of the invaders. Dirk called in four P-51 Mustang fighter planes of the U.S.

The streaking down planes tore up the rebel forces, and strafed their camps near the border. An end was put to the invasion.

The weapons provided to the Guardia from our cargo proved effective in the holding phase of the invasion. Time to do more was gained. The volunteers proved the Ticos were ready to die for freedom, but they could not do effective battle with trained soldiers. The Guardia did much better, but it was still under armed.

"We need to go up to Guatemala and pick up a cargo of military weapons for the Guardia. They have a lot of new men who have come in." Dirk decided.

We were aboard the "Flying Kate" once again. The Captain was happy going down the Gulf of Nicoya and out on to the surging sea. We all felt a sense of freedom from the complicated modern world. The water world was vast and clean. It absorbed our black plume of smoke quite easily. The Captain said it was the trail of our sins going out over the white wake of our lives.

The sea had a tendency to run hard off the Guanacaste coast. The ship did some plunging in the stormy seas. We had adjusted to ship motion. Even Sporty had gotten his sea legs, and had earned the title of "C.I.A. SEA DOG" over his deck house.

Dirk was studying the Nicaragua coastline with the binoculars. He found we were being observed.

The marketers in Guatemala were happy to fill our hold with the latest military hardware. The "Flying Kate" was heavy in the water with the stuff of war. We turned our portside to the land, and voyaged down the coastline.

Off Nicaragua shells came whistling in, and sending spurts of water up around us. Sporty ran below, Matt started to curse in the galley, and the Captain veered off to sea to make the ship a small target. Steve turned his cannon to stern. He blasted the trees along the shoreline. There was silence.

We did not repair the shell hole in Matt's galley. It provided better ventilation. But it got his ire up that it was there. He came from a world where it was an insult to be shot at.

"You can look out at the sea while cooking." we told him.

We heard a bang in the galley. Matt had flattened a roach. He had a special pot for it. The God Cook always brought swift justice to any of Satan's little buggers who dared invade his galley world.

"Keep it out of our soup." Steve hollered.

Incidents at sea bring back sharp memories. It must be the sea air that does it. It brought me back to thinking about a thing of the pots. I was at Berkeley when Reagan had his helicopters up over the heads of the students from the Commie bookstores. The police were rapping the students on the head with their clubs. You know Reagan. Stand tall and attack. I was fortunate to have the Press card to prevent a flat head. The students were too poor to buy helmets. They used pots from the kitchen! "This cop hit me hard," on student complained to me, "My ears were ringing for days afterward." Funny, and sad too.

The Guardia was growing all the time....many more members. In Costa Rica it was sort of a gauge to measure the violence of the world.

The world will not let you have a police force. It forces you to get an Army. That is the sad story of man's doing all along his history.

Steve was happy with the expanding Guardia. He liked uniforms and guns. If it could be made into an Army, he would work to go up the ranks to a commanding position.

Chapter 14

The events of our years in Costa Rica were like a kaleidoscope. Many and varied experiences hung loose in a procedure toward a Social Democracy. What was hoped for was ever elusive. The social programs moved beyond the basic. Trouble!

The country was like a beautiful bunch of grapes on a vine in a Paradise. The expensive social programs turned some of the grapes sour. Economy is the lifeblood of any nation. The easygoing people wanted better living even though they could not pay for it. Coffee, and then bananas, fitted the bill for a time, prior to development. Then came the short falls.

Instead of the simple living advanced by the Captain, the Legislators turned to the deadly passions of lust and greed to solve their growing economic problems. The Tourist Trade offered plenty of paying people to support the Democracy Dream. "Come to our Paradise of climate, birds, and flowers!" the Ticos offered the world. They needed to attract a lot of the tourists in. Places of sin in a Paradise would do it. So lax laws allowed illicit sex houses, motels that rent by the hour, casinos, high-rise hotels, red-light districts full of hard luck whores, call girls for the wealthy, many and various tourist stays and tours in nature places, volcano roads up, and unwise developments of concrete in malls and parking places, plus many roads and cars running all over the countryside. Sleazy and funky stay places sprang up like mushrooms so hippie-type people could come in, and then go on to establish their colonies. The Nicoya Peninsula offered a lot of space for escapees from California to gravitate down.

"Come and do it!" was the hippie battle cry.

The corrupting way of the world, in time, would cause the good things to drop off the vine like withered grapes. It was understandable that the Legislators did not want their names involved in a book. It was the old story of man ruining a Paradise. Even now, early in development, signs of future decline were in the offing. The Formers of the society choose to ignore them. Times were booming! There is bust in the boom.

The Time of Ending is the time of no room. Costa Rica is a tiny place. The worst thing that can happen to it are hordes of people.

They did need the Captain as their President. He wisely declined to get involved in the affairs of men who would pursue money instead of spiritual living. He knew the course a Presidency would take into conflicts and confusions. It takes all men to do something, not just one. The Ticos would not bridle their sex for any distant goal. They were for dipping into a fleshpot despite working a marriage at home. He did not want to get into the middle between the ends. The practice of sex in the wrong ways would help unravel the fabric of society in time. Not to mention gamblings. Not to mention the Tech monster about to straddle the society. He knew they would not follow his directions. He knew. But they were good at peace. He advised them to start a University of Peace in the world. Contradictions come from not understanding the illusions of the earth plane. Such situations can breed even worse children among men. There are many unseen ghosts going around in the Times of Last.

Matt took up a cook position at the Gran Hotel downtown. Soon the legislators were eating lunch there. Near the General Assembly. The place became popular with tourists too.

"There is our lifeblood." One legislator said to another. "They will fill our coffers with the gold we do not have in our ground. Let us build forward!"

"Who is the excellent cook?" another asked.

"He belongs to the Captain. Off the "Flying Kate" ship. A rather famous Chicago gangster of the Al Capone days."

"Is the soup safe?"

"Don't know. But it sure is good!"

"These Italians are excellent cooks. Trained by their mamas in the ways of seductive foods. Runs in the family. The Captain made a good find. Keeps his crew together too."

The Captain was busy with University talks, and going to diplomatic and legislative parties. He worked hard to spread his positive influence around in all quarters, trying to give right direction to those forming the society. "Think into the future." He advised all.

Ted got to work reorganizing the library at the University. He was also acting principal at a large high school. "Books are my children." he told us. "I have to take care of them, so they can take care of the kids."

Matt was making the legislators fat.

Steve was working to streamline the Guardian Civil, and extend better ways and methods of applying force in a velvet glove—out to the growing web of Rural Guardia in the developing towns along the newly paved roads.

Willy was just hanging out with the students at the University.

I was just making notes, and sitting around wondering where it all was going. And, quietly, being the Captain's secret weapon. I kept Dirk's big secrets, and the Captain's small ones. The Captain's small big secret is the he drinks only ginger ale at the cocktail parties. His big secret is that Lenora is his Achilles heel.

Everyone was so busy that Willy just slipped out of our protective fingers. I am ashamed to admit it. The hippies got him.! He was ripe for this. We did not notice it. Lacking the excitement of fire, and being for peace, they made him a flower child and led him into their debacle. He got lost in their world of debauchery. It took Steve to rescue him.

Willy heard of the Columbus Day blowout called a festival that exploded in sleepy Puerto Limon each year. Some student passed the excitement to him, and he had to go.

"I'm going to see IT." he insisted. He was going!

"All right," I said. "I'll go with you, Willy."

We went up over the mountain range, and down to the hot jungle coast. Puerto Limon was in a frenzy of activity in the form of floats, noisy bands blaring in the streets, and Indians, Chinese, and Africans, painted up from head to toe, dancing wildly in the streets. Near naked, and drunk, they moved to a seductive drumbeat. Fireworks exploded in the sky. Fermentations of anything made up the fiery liquors. Combined with the beat they drive men into madness. Dance yourself to death. Ticos came by the hundreds to do it too. It was a scene from the wild side of Costa Rica.

Willy grabbed a drink, and put it down. "Fire!" he yelled. "I Want to Dance!"

A female student latched on to him, after he had more drinks. She took him to meet Jimmy LoveSex—the Guru from California, Who Can Make It Right For You.

I tried to interfere, but Willy was in some sort of reaction to no longer being an arsonist. There was no holding him back. He was on a heavy kick.

The hippie guru invited Willy to his colony being formed on the Nicoya Peninsula—so he could learn to live with flowers in his mind and hair too. He was to be reborn. His female follower dragged Willy off the street into a funky room.

"Damn it," I exclaimed, "I need Steve here!"

Finally I took a forlorn Willy home. He was whacked out—and in.

It all seemed to pass easy. But then the female student came to take Willy on a visit to the great guru and his settlement forming. He stayed on there.

Soon Willy was doing moon howls in the naked. He was in the nudity circle where the ganja smoke hung heavy. He took to smoking some stuff. He was doing Shakespeare's "beast with two backs", and not even knowing he had a partner. He was a gone guy. Now the fire had become mental and within.

Fifty naked hippies hit the fruit groves of a large Catholic church one night, out near a town in the countryside. They laid their girls under the trees, and took fruit down too to eat. It became a Sodom and Gomorrah scene.

The "good father" heard the commotion. He took his bird gun and flashlight down off the shelf. He took a young novice with him for protection. He turned on the flashlight, and directed it under the trees.

"What are they doing, father?" the young man asked.

"If you don't know I'm not going to be the one to tell you….and away from here we must go!" the priest replied, hurrying the novice away from the orchard.

Steve got mad. He knew Willy had been under the trees with the wild bunch.

"They are not going to keep carrying on in my territory. I'm going to get Willy back here." he said in a huff.

He came roaring into the settlement, and braked the vehicle to a stop in a cloud of dust. He then collared the guru….took him by the neck.

"Your withered leg does not get you any tolerance with me. Your damn brain is withered too. You had better inhibit your people. When I'm out on the patrol ship at night, I can overshoot an invading boat and blow your damn camp all to hell! Do you get me? I want you to cut Willy loose within a week, and get my brother back into my crew."

Willy was back within a week. He had tales to tell.

"That Jimmy Love really did it. Tico girls and guys coming in had to do sex with him. He said it was the only way into the spiritual circle of the God Guru. He said he was the Love in the universe. They all did it."

"What crap!" Steve said. "Willy, your right place is with us. I'm going to put the damper on those people. We do not need downers from California fouling up the Peninsula. They are going to find it hard going from now on."

"One awful stormy night the guru came running down the dirt road naked and screaming. His eyes were bugging out awful. His long black locks were hanging down, and dripping in the rain pouring down. The glare of lightning flashes made him look like a devil from hell. He looked like Charley Manson. He scared me awful." Willy confided in us.

Willy wanted me to do a poem for him about his sojourn into the hippie world. He said he wanted it to hang on his wall back home in Oak Lawn. It had been an amazing and awful experience. "O.K. Willy," I agreed "Tell me all about it." I had never used any dope, except coffee.

THE HIP PEOPLE

We were the people Hip
Who knew we were in the know
And we took many a wild LSD trip
Living like a wily old black crow

We hit the road
Under the dark goad

Traveled far and near
Traveled far and near
Doing the things that made the soul seer

We ate the carrots in the field
And all else the countryside would yield
We filled our sacks full of farts
And put LSD in our brownies and tarts

Went right thru the crack between the worlds
And ran screaming from all sorts of dire perils
Went into the dark woods
And were chased by red-eyed devils
Whose white fangs shone beneath black hoods

Doping and screwing was our thing
We had a wild and wicked fling
Named the Devil Jack of Hearts
For ours were his in those days of lore
Even Poe's raven came to croak around us…
Nevermore!

We danced with spirits and devils
Till they came to bury us with shovels
Then we ran away
And found a place to pray

We danced with Don Juan and his demons
While their eyes cast out baleful beamins
Because he was a cool cat
And knew it was our hour
We tasted of the Dark Power

By LSD we made a hell of our own
In which we could scream and groan

We danced with demons in the shadowy glens
And spent time behind bars in the city pens
But we took LSD and it made us free
And we stood in the prairies to pee
Strange sights did we see
LSD LSD LSD

The stars were our father and mother
We had no other
We slept out on the sod
And LSD was our God

Had all sorts of dreamins
Done all sorts of schemings
Took a lot of reamings
Did hip high beamings

LSD was our God….and it put some of us under the sod

In the tombs by the sea
We went in and shook the skeletons
To get up and take LSD
We said—It's for thee
That you might like us see

We slept with them and rattled their bones
Coming out of LSD they heard our groans
And at times we heard their moans
Then we all went out to shout at the sounding sea
And off the dark cliffs there we did pee

Up to the Catholic church we did flee
Fifty naked in the moonlight…We…Whee
A raid upon the church's orchard was made

Under its trees our girls were laid

Suddenly in the dark of night came on a flashlight bright
Upon our doping, fruiting, and screwing
A young brother asked the old father...."What are they doing?"
He replied....“If you don’t know, I’m not the one to tell you and
Away we must go....”

So there then we took our trip
And it was a pip: Oh, mad moon so staring bright in the night—eye of
An evil God
Did obscene (and howling) at the full moon shining
And finally fell under the trees pining
To greet the dawn reclining

We danced naked in a little country church
And used the altar for our perch
Two women came in
To give up some sin
They fainted dead away
And must remember the scene to this day
Nevermore will they enter that church door

Now we are the squares on your home block
Who live by the clock
Now we live to get the pay
Yea Yea
To live comfortable day by day
Yea Yea
For all must get the pay

It was too much LSD for you and me

Now our thoughts won't jell
So many of our stories we can not tell
About the making of our private hell

We see the squares smoke a bit of pot
Then they think they are real hot
We give each other the nudge
And think to put some real stuff in their fudge
But it's the pay that saves their day

To those who would go weird
Let us forbid
Lest you be dood
Like we been did
NEVERMORE!

"That's it! That's it!" Willy said, "You got it! There was one guy who turned blue and never came back. They did away with him somewhere...don't know where. It's bad over there."

Steve snickered and snickered. "That damn guru! I should destroy that nest of roaches. Just like Matt with his special pot. I have my cannon. But Dirk won't let me do it. Those foul people will go on to establish a community on the Nicoya Peninsula. It's remote enough so they can get away with it. Perhaps we could inject some of the howler monkeys with rabies, and turn them loose on those roaches....I'd give anything to find that body."

"Thank Steve for saving you, Willy." Ted said.

"I sure do give thanks to Steve. It's bad there. Never would have got out of there on my own." Willy agreed.

"This poem is a classic. It opens a window on a world we should know about, but never go in. It's the dark side of civilization." Ted told me. "Get it published."

"There's no money in Poetry. Nor is this world worth bothering with. It's full of pooits and arty posers. I have done near one hundred poems just out of love of writing. They are on their own. If they can live in time, God Bless them." I replied.

"The classic writers of the past always started with poetry." Ted pointed out. "It's the way to put inspirations into short form."

"By the way," I said. "Don't tell the Captain I wrote 'The Hip People.'"

While having lunch at the outdoor café downtown, Jessica came up to me. She wanted to know about the Captain. She is the daughter of a diplomat, and had been seeing the Captain at the parties going on at high level. Tall, dark, and beautiful she had been the Coffee Queen, and had been involved in other beauty vanities at the University. Her ego was as high as her outward physical appearance.

"I've been told you are writing the Captain's life story. He is such a mysterious man. But what a man! I'm thinking of marrying him. Tell me what he is like. I have heard the fantastic story of that voyage around the Horn." she said, and added, "He loves me."

"The Captain loves everyone." I informed her. "It's his nature."

"Yes, he seems to go for Maria too. She goes to the parties. She came up from the mud floor of an adobe hut to the luxurious house of one of the Presidents. We have a lot of Presidents since they can only have one term. I do not like the idea of sharing his love with others."

"You do not understand. He is a spiritual lover. He loves many."

"I can make him forget the others."

"Not possible. But you need to know that there is someone else from the world of women who is special to him—extremely special. A goddess!"

Her face fell.

"Someone else? Who? Where?"

"Leonora"

"Where?"

"Beyond"

"Oh?"

"Sorry to say, she is a goddess who was his worldly love in the past. Now gone physically, but never spiritually. Behind the Command Confidence Sea Captain there is a lover pining away. It is so sad to see. She is his soul mate. Lovely, desirable, and sadly lost."

"You said is?"

"For him, yes!"

"I can make him forget her."

"Don't try, for your own sake." I warned her. "No one can duplicate a goddess. A substitute will not work."

"Sounds like a romantic novel. It seems unreal."

"It's real enough. I have heard him crying quietly in his cabin at sea. I am deeply worried about him."

"Why would you be like that?"

"His crew is within the circle of his special love. We love him too."

"Sounds a bit fruity."

"Definitely not! He is a spiritual man. Such a man can't be understood by natural man. The natural man does not have the capacity to know the spiritual. His love is beyond the worldly type. We are most fortunate to be his crew. He is a great man. That is why I choose to be his secret weapon, and tell the world his life story. Such a story must not be gone with the wind in life. The good things in Costa Rica will go, but his story will not go. I can understand your desire for him. He is the dream man of all lonely girls the world over. At least they will have his story….and they will keep him alive down the ages."

"That's too much for me. I hope I can give him my body without getting too involved. He told me about the Seventh heaven, which I now understand. We will visit it. Then I will have to think of him as a ship sailing off to the vast sea."

"Bless you." I said, to put the period at the end of the sentence.

Sporty had his own version of love. Matt came to the ship on his day off for "some sun, sea, and sand." He had his folding chair up, and was dozing on the stern. Sporty peed on his leg. He jumped up yelling, "What is this? What is this?" I told him that Sporty had reversed his psychology.

"He hates me?" Matt thought.

"On the contrary," I offered, "He is marking his territory. You are his meal ticket. He has claimed you as his own. He loves you."

"Well, I've not had much love in my life." Matt admitted. "I have to take what comes along."

He reached down and patted Sporty. The happy dog wiggled wildly. More than his tail, his whole back end was wiggling around. Sporty was an all out loving dog.

On the ship, the Captain called up one of his three-lessons teaching sessions. They were always full of sharp points, rather rememorable. His objective was the dispensation of wisdom to live by...which he called Common Sense. It was part of the Sea Change the Hometown Four were sailing in. Our uniforms were for physical grounding on a tight ship. The sessions were part of the mental discipline. Love was the spiritual discipline. It added up to Command Confidence for each of us.

He was devious in his teachings. Analysis was always required. He told us we were mental miners, and had to dig for our gold. Sometimes the gold was near the surface, sometimes very deep.

"The First One: A man was put in an insane asylum for a terrible murder. They asked him why he did such a horrible thing. 'God told me to do it.' He replied. 'I did not!' the man standing next to him yelled out. Why did I put this one first? Vanity is the most dangerous of the deadly passions because it causes all the others. Beware of acting like you are God. Think!

The Second One: Again an insane asylum. The lunatic fringe of society offers some great learnings for those who do not live on it. It is debatable as to who does live on it. All is relative. The time is World War I. World War is the untrue phenomena of the universal lunatic fringe of man. Soldiers are running past the institution, and bombs are bursting in the air. An inmate runs to the window. 'Look at all those crazy fools killing each other out there!' he yells. This is the historic state of society. Think a lot more on this in all the ramifications involved.

The Third One: Two men are in a deep discussion about a friend named Dunn. One said he had been talking with the mother on the phone, and had promised her he would get the son to write to her. So he went around inquiring where Dunn was presently. He moved around a lot in New York city. No one knew his whereabouts. Finally he saw the sign Dunn and Bradstreet on a building. He went in and asked for Dunn. A wag there said he was in the toilet. He saw a man sitting on the toilet. "Are you Dunn?" he inquired. "Yes, I am done." was the answer. "WRITE YOUR MOTHER!!!" In the phantasmagoria of the flux in this world of the earth plane it is easy to be mistaken. Are the Ticos correct in eliminating the death penalty? Make applications of this joke in your personal life too."

"Captain, you are a joker!" Steve said.

"I've been speaking especially to you, Steve. Joke and no joke. You have been walking over the edge of violence. It's not a good place to be. Some of your doings were forced necessary, but you are inclined to go beyond. Temper yourself. Your mistakes can cost lives. Would you really want to blow those poor wayward hippie people away?"

He knew about my poem.

The Captain told us we should visit the Friend's Meeting House at Montverde. Something good had come out of Fairhope, Alabama. A group of 41 Quakers came to establish a community in Costa Rica because it had no Army. He said we should have a high respect for these peacemakers, and encourage their society. Remember our Lesson Two.

We found them building roads, and buildings, and a cheese factory up on a plateau. Not far from San Jose, and a good climate place for an agrarian society to locate. They bid us welcome.

We sat in silence in their Meeting House.

A few Quakers got up and gave testimonials from the spirit in their lives. Interesting accounts better than from most life-livers in the world. Something was working for good.

Finally the Captain rose up to speak. He expressed his love for all. They were eager to hear him out. Love and peace are words the Quakers relish. Good people!

"My crew and I live in a world of love, which we keep detached from the general world of men and their deadly passions. I know that you wisely do the same in your community. We are kin. It is commendable that you have historically managed to overcome the first deadly passion of anger that leads to murders and horrible wars. You also manage to tone down the remaining four passions. Costa Ricans have also conquered the first, but the others are threatening to get them. This tiny nation is the only one among the nations that has moved up beyond the first. No Army, and no death penalty. The citizens do not believe in confrontations in personal life either. They have moved away from direct physical violence. That is why you are in this country. Good! Bless you all. Live in Peace."

"You are in the spirit. We have heard that you came here to work for peace, and that makes us brothers." A leading Quaker spoke up. "Silence is for welcoming the spirit in. We do love to talk about Peace in the world with those willing to hear of it."

"We follow the Prince of Peace." Lamont stated, and continued on...."You avoid smoking and drinking which are so prevalent among the population. It is wise. We do too. No need to burn out God's holy temple. Pray in it instead.

The people here have much more to learn. They are sinking in the swamp of sex. The second deadly passion is getting them, and it will go on to the third too. Lust is a pastime here. Greed will cause those in power to put up high-rise tourist hotels that will ruin the land and the sea at the beaches. Bahia Culebra is a huge bay of deep water and tremendous beauty in the north. I've heard that some developer-minded leaders here already see its potential for money. Greed can cause ruin. To save the nation you ruin the nation. A wrong procedure. Here is a Paradise between the Oceans and the Continents of butterflies and orchids in which animals and flowers flourish. Man finds delights in living here. Only man can turn it into a Paradise Lost. As a backer and promoter of Democracy we urge you to preach protection of the environment. Simple living is the key."

"We are simple people here." an old Quaker replied.

"The makes you complicated in the eyes of the world." Lamont said with a laugh "The world wonders what you are up to."

"Just Peace."

"No more horrors of war!"

"That, and serenity in the soul."

"Burn all the flags, bury all the guns, pee on all the uniforms preferably with the generals in them." The Captain offered.

"We like your humor, Captain. You speak like a salty old sea dog."

"That's what I am." The Captain declared. "Just an old dog of the sea."

"Not so." I spoke up. "You are in the presence of a great man—a really great man!"

"And you are....?" one asked.

"The one who is writing his life story. I would urge you to read it. It is full of amazing insights. Its title will be 'The Sea Change.'"

"Our community takes high interest in a peace-maker. We will read."

We continued driving on to the northwest to check out some towns along the growing web of pothole roads. Conditions were poor in the remote area. The roads of Costa Rica seemed to have been made by sozzolled map-makers for manic drivers bent on suicide. Pouring from gas cans took the place of no gas stations. You pay double or sit on a dirt road. Willy would yell out "Here comes the guy with the gas can!" Dingy rooms and poor meals. We choose Matt for food, and the vehicle to sleep in. Out in the remote it was always a rough go for us.

The Captain, Willy, Matt, and I took shelter under the huge umbrella-like Guanacaste tree. Its shade was welcome to ward off the hot sun. We shared it with a bunch of cattle, which stayed on their side.

Matt spread out a blanket for a tree picnic. Out of the cooler chest came his delights for our food. He had cold drinks for us too. We dined in Paradise with the animals. The cattle watched us with a wary eye, not knowing we were in Paradise.

The Captain was stately, as always, but had on open shirt and jeans. He did an undress after the Quaker Meeting. The natty appearance and debonair mien were gone. Those were for the cocktail parties and the slinky women of Monte Carlo who tried to capture him like a prize fish. They would suffer humiliation if they knew he favored the lonely young widows mainly. He took delight in gracing the lives of the lonely. His inspirative loving caused them to seek a new husband for the kids. They came back to a positive condition of being. Our good Captain!

"We have Clark Gable with us." Willy said. "He should be in the movies!"

The Captain laughed, and raised his glass of ginger ale to salute our picnic with him. A picnic we all would remember. He took delight in small talk, and the telling of clean jokes. It was his way to relax and be with his crew.

I remembered a little joke from our Marine newspaper at the Tontoua Air Base in New Caledonia. Could not resist giving it a try on him.

"Captain, I was editor of the notorious 'Ton-tooter', Marine newspaper, New Caledonia, War II. Here comes a gem from the file. It is one of the mild ones. See if you like it."

Mary's Watch

Mary had a little watch
She swallowed it one day
Now she's drinking castor oil
….to pass the time away.
Oh, the oil did not work
The watch did not pass.
If you want to know the time
Just look up Mary's….Uncle.
He's gotta watch!"

"That's a neat one. It's tricky, especially at the end!" Lamont laughed.

"The end! You put a great end to the poem. May it rest in peace too." I replied. I like your two-liner you tacked up on the ship's bridge at the Horn better.

The waters are wild today
It would be wise to pray"

"If you don't stop the poetry stuff it's going to drive me to join The Flat Earth Society." Matt informed us. "How can I think with you guys around?"

"Think?" Willy said. "You mean stink."

"All right, Willy, Don't fool with the cook. He can do us all in." Lamont said. "Brother Matt is our joy and keeps us going. We love him."

We drove on to view Bahia Culebra from the land. Previously, the ship had taken anchorage there to stop boats from Nicaragua running down the Golfo de Papagayo. At this part of the sea, so deep, but locked in by land, the Captain stood overlooking the huge waters. He seemed perturbed. I heard him saying something…

"It's the sea, but Golfo Dulce has a sweet name, and Cabo Matapalo faces the open Pacific and the waves come in from thousands of miles to the West."

On the way back toward San Jose, we stopped at Tabacon hot Springs close by the Arenal Volcano. Waterfalls came down from the heights. We soaked in the mineral waters amid lush scenery. The Captain relaxed so much he went to sleep…and we had to awaken him to view the fiery display of the Volcano.

Chapter 15

We made a stop at Puntarenas. Juan was at the dock with his fast speedboat that served the nation as patrol boat. He had changed much from his former simple self. He wore a uniform that Dirk had inspired. He was prosperous with a new house built that even had electricity, and a paved road in front of it. He appeared extremely nervous.

"My other son watches over your ship well," he informed us, "But my oldest son is hanging out with those hippie people. He is smoking some stuff that stuns him. We are much worried about him."

"Sorry to hear that." The Captain said. "Perhaps he should talk with Steve some?"

"He is going his own way in pursuit of the pleasures, and will not listen to anyone." Juan replied. "He will soon be lost to us."

"Any trouble out on patrol?"

"Oh Yes! Stopped two boats after dusk. They had Nics in them. I had to put the machine gun in their faces to turn them around. I followed them back up to the border."

"My brother Al would have made Swiss cheese out of them. He was in that business." Matt informed Juan.

"How are you doing Juan, in your new life?" the Captain inquired. "Does it suit you, make you happy?"

"Money is nice. But now I get nervous, and drink, and have two girl friends. The Mala Monkey comes after me when midnight passes. We should blow up Isla Chirra. My wife has a room full of saints she prays to....for our son and me. Does no good."

"Being a Captain of a boat is good." Lamont stated. "You can relax out at sea much of the time, Juan. Do you do it?"

"Some," he said, "But ashore the tourists are after me to take them to women and to find Quetzal birds to watch. They come here for this, you know. They bother the monkeys and the wild jumpers throw things at them, crap on them when they are under the trees, and steal their belongings left on the beaches. The monkeys are no longer happy here."

"Neither are you, Juan. Look how you think and talk. Just like a modern man of the fouled up world."

"Yes," Juan replied, "I do not know what is happening anymore. We had little before, but much more too. Now I can see it. But you can't go back. Perhaps I should go live in San Jose?"

"That would only make things worse for you." Lamont warned.

Dirk called us into session in San Jose. He revealed a promotional plan he was working on to use the ship. It was an important C.I.A. asset.

"We have lost much of our hidden quality now. Let's take the ship to ports in the U.S. as a movie ship. We will promote tourism to Costa Rica. The famous ship of the Horn. Show a movie aboard of the Paradise. Pass out bottles with messages in them...come and help save the birds, the flowers, and the animals in paradise. You know, some nations have sent funds to establish Reserves and Parks in Costa Rica. They want to preserve Paradise. It is man's eternal dream that has come down the ages. We can capitalize on this. We will help them to help us. This can be done well. What do you think on this?"

"Sounds good" we agreed.

"Present status of Operation Goodheart is good. Thanks to us Democracy is a going reality here. But what the government is doing with it is another matter. We are not getting all hoped for. And the waves of drug abuse and of terrorism are now running on the surface of the Dark Ocean of life here. This tiny spot is between forces, and it is getting to be a hot one. Money will have to be spent on counter measures."

"When do we go?" Ted asked.

"It will be soon." Dirk replied vaguely.

It was only a few days later that Dirk called us in for a meeting.

"Steve is dead!" he informed us. "A fer de lance struck him up in the remote area of the swamps, lagoons, and canals. Some rebels were fooling around there. He went to ferret them out. He did not make it to the hospital in time. Died right at its door. Now you are the Hometown Three."

I felt sad. He had been my bad buddy in life. Never to me, but to others. Now gone.

The Captain had tears in his eyes. He said nothing.

"That terrible snake is the Devil's own pet. Sorry it happened." Dirk said.

"The wind blew him across Tennyson's Bar." Ted said. "Just as it will, in our own time, do so to each of us."

"Where is that Bar?" Willy wanted to know.

"It's in the Shoals of Satan on the shore of the Dark Ocean...waiting for all men. Death is a prime weapon of the Evil One, and the enemy of mankind. We are fragile. We are subject to it for sure. The Dark Power rules over the physical world. It's revealed in the classical rendition of man's thought." Ted replied.

"Be of good cheer." The Captain told us. "The Correcting Coming is near. Life will triumph. Man was not made for death, but for life. You can sense this at your core. Love well in life, and fret not. We will say a prayer for our Steve, as is our way in the crew."

I knew the Captain had been struck hard in his heart. Yet what he said was true. Eden would be restored finally, not in Costa Rica, but over the whole earth plane. He would be with his Lenora again.

Matt just sat. He had witnessed much bloody murder. He had seen many go. The Dark Power was no stranger to him. He felt helpless. Steve was just gone. Soon he would be too. Steve had been the strong man among us.

"Damn it!" Dirk lamented, "We should just chuck it all, and go back to Ushuaia. The only safe city is in Patagonia, at the end of the world. Look at the sorry state of the world. The nations are in turmoil Our efforts come to naught. Do you remember those brightly painted buildings spread out at the foot of snowy mountains with the sea in the front yard? Clean air, clean water, and good seafood. Nice people too. We should have stayed there."

"The dream of Paradise even in Dirk!" the Captain said, "But that large island between the tip of South America and the Horn is a place of stormy weather and penguins. Four kinds of penguins: There is a rockhopper penguin, a chinstrap penguin, a king penguin, and a macaroni penguin. The macaroni penguin comes from Italy. My point is that it is a place of penguins there. And so rocky! Do you remember the williwaws? How our Sporty got hit with icy stones from out of the howling winds? How we were turned over? Here it is lush. Full of flowers. Colorful birds. Everything is lush and colorful here. You can choose what climate you will have. The government is gentle too. Seldom is there much of an overcast. A sunny clime!"

"Yes, but thousands of penguins all dressed up, and no place to go. We should go back and give them a big party....so they will have a place to go. Everyone should have a place to go." Willy said.

"The plight of the penguins! Those hippies did something to our Willy. Left him a sec fiend too. Notice he goes after the little girls now. But they can run faster than him, except a few." Ted insighted.

The Captain brought us back to the mundane mode. "Steve was a great asset to the Guardia. They will surely miss him. He saved us a couple of times on our perilous voyage too. Let us remember him with thanks."

We all decided to watch our step in Paradise.

"Let the nations watch their step too." Dirk added.

Chapter 16

Matt had been working on his image. From the Swiss cheese mode of existence, he hit out for the top of society. His mid life in the crew with the Captain was the best of all, but he failed to see it so. He wanted to be with the arty posers at the top of things. His brother Al had rubbed shoulders with them, while buying them off. The pillars of society are rather shaky. Yet they appear so fine. Matt was a man of the short view. The chef position at the Gran Hotel filled him full of airs.

I came across him at the downtown outdoor lunch spot. He was wearing a tam, and had a long cigarette holder. He had on the latest clothes. T-shirt days were over. His white shoes were a legacy of Al. Al had considered them arrival shoes, and had topped himself with a white hat and white suit….bring whiteness to dispel the blackness. Matt followed the precedent of Al. He was decked out to impress the legislators at lunch. He had Sporty with him on a fancy leash. Sporty was clean, combed, and happy. He was probably anticipating the ice cream cones Matt would provide at times. Matt told us he had a girl going to beauty school who groomed Sporty in her practice. We had given Sporty into Matt's care because Juan's son did not take much care of him on the ship anchored in the remote cove.

"Matt!" I exclaimed. "Are you going nuts?"

"Sir, do not use such vulgar language in my presence. I am Mattiste Caparonelli, the chef of the Royal Governors who direct the course of this important nation. My food is the foundation of the Government."

"They are only elected officials." I replied.

"Humph. You fail to understand who they are."

Sporty wiggled beside me. He shoved his nose under my hand to get a petting. Matt threw up his hand at the dog's behavior. He told me he was sorry to see Steve go.

Willy was sitting around perplexed by Steve being snaked out of existence. He was upset by the happening. He went to the Captain for some understanding of it.

"It's the Law of Karma operating in the phantasmagoria of the flux."

"The Who? The What?" Willy reacted.

"Steve attracted violence to himself by doing violence. Near the border he caused a scene of dead, dying, and wounded rebels. Fired a shotgun full of 00 buck at the gravel in front of them. What we see is the ghostly procession of change on the earth plane. The Greeks just had a fancy way of describing it. Change is the great principle operating in life. It allows us to become better, to advance....toward the greatness in the unseen. You will always see things changing."

"Some men have tried to make things remain the same." Willy observed.

"That's the Bed of Procrustes. The Greeks conceived of a giant who took travelers and forced them to fit his iron bed....stretch them if short and cut them off if long. This reveals what dictators are like. There will be an ultimate one. May you not be there when he comes on stage."

Dirk told the Captain to prepare the ship for a voyage back to Wilmington Harbor at San Pedro in California. Back to old haunts to pick up a cargo of special supplies needed in Costa Rica. The deal had been made. Boxed up materials. Secret. We were all to go along, so no new crew would be needed. A leave would be arranged for Matt; so he could be our cook.

The voyage up the coast is not a long one. It is a rather amiable section of the sea. The sun shines nicely, and the waves behave well. Seldom is there a heavy storm. To our Captain it was more than welcome. He took a deep breath, threw his arms out, and embraced the sea. He put Willy at the wheel of the helm, so he could get up in the bow and breathe in the sea air and get the gentle wind in his face. He was always happy to leave the land. Sporty came and sat by his side. Another sea dog.

The sun shone brightly, and the waters washed in peaked whiteness around us. The immense circle of sea and sky gave us a sense of space and freedom from the earth with its webs of complexities created by men. There was always the sense of openness and being free from complications out at sea. It dissolved the fuming of Matt caused by his being diverted from the hotel back to the ship.

The afterglow of sunset deepened into night. Then in the soft hush of the silence the thousands of concaves of the sea surface reflected the moonlight in shining splendor. Magical night at sea. It was a time of awe. The Captain was in his element. His ship was a living thing related to the universe of the water world.

Lamont looked at the sea. He said: "Our mother." The smell of the open sea was clean, and it gave new life to the spirit. He called us to prayer—and it was beautiful, private, and inspiring to the crew. Our prayer was always alive, and special to us. The essence of the sea was in it. The Captain took his delight in it. We became sea entities. It was left for ordinary mortals to be just sea men.

There it was—the entrance to the channel, off San Pedro. Lights were twinkling on ashore. The ship moved down the channel like a shadow. The anchor rattled to the bottom in front of the dock. We had come full circle. Only Steve was missing....

After dawn, Matt went ashore and took up residence in the same motel as Randolph Hunter. He like that name. So did I as a writer. It had sort of a romance power in it. Matt had a few surprising things in him.

While we were loading cargo, two U.S. Marshals came to the motel and took Matt into custody. The thin owner looked over his glasses at the officers, heard the name Matthew Capone, and fell to the floor in a faint. He remembered the violent argument in his motel between Matt and Steve.

Dirk tried to interfere....no use. Matt was wanted by the Kefauver Senate Investigating Committee, meeting at the old courthouse in Chicago, for questioning pertaining to his brother Al. He had to go.

"It's O.K., Matt." I tried to comfort him. "You are getting a free ride back to Chicago. We will have to pay for it."

"They are going to make me into a bum again." he complained. We felt sorry for him.

Sporty disappeared. The officers assumed he was Matt's dog. In time I found out that one of them took Sporty home so he "could play with the kids." A damn dognapper! But Sporty would have a good home. When he would be asleep, and his leg would twitch, and he would make strange noises, the kids would wonder why. He would be dreamin of his past adventures on a voyage with a fabulous Captain and a crew that loved him. Few people have ever had the excitements of his past. A good Captain. A lucky dog. Old age with loving kids isn't too bad. But he would never forget us.

After his release from the Courthouse questioning, Matt did not go back on the street by the Midwest Hotel. He used his new name and props to secure a chef position at the Drake Hotel. He made them a dish to try. They took him at face value, and hired him on. He did wonderful work there for a month. Then someone checked on him—and he was fired. Two years later he put a gun to his head. He was taken to Mt Carmel to finally be with brother Al. Anyway, the Sea Change did work for awhile for him.

We brought the cargo back to Puntarenas. It was unloaded and taken by railroad to San Jose. Dirk took care of it. He never told us what we were hauling by sea. He was sorry about Matt....Matt had helped the C.I.A. in small ways. That is what Dirk told us in time. He never did say how...and we were unable to fit it back in. Our lives were a jigsaw puzzle that only the C.I.A. could put together because they had all the parts.

At the Gran Hotel the staff asked us about Matt. We told them.

"Fools!" the manager exclaimed. "A great chef is hard to find!"

We agreed that they had struck out in the U.S., when it came to Matt. Brother Al had cast too long a shadow. Mt. Carmel is not a good ending for the family: only monuments.

The Captain and I sat down in the park near the National Theater. We wanted to sum up where we had come to now. The many birds were being happy in the trees. They filled the air with their whistling, screeching, and chattering. The feathery flight world in Paradise is quite vocal....and even more colorful. Living flying colors in green trees.

"Does the bird sound bother you?" I asked.

"No, it is to me like the monkeys on the mirror. But alive and yet simple too."

"Our crew has been cut short by life." I observed.

"I still have you, Willy, and Ted. You know, Sporty was one of the crew too. He is better off in a home with kids. That's all right. We will miss him, however. The Sea Change was working well for Matt until negation came to foul it up for him. The past can sometimes become the future. We were his only good time in life. God Bless him. Steve never responded well to change. I agree with you it was his nasty mother. Willy is doing O.K. Ted seems stable enough."

"Yes, he did a good thing to take refuge in books when his wife died early of a heart attack in town. I used to kid him that he had doubled his trouble in life, but he was devoted her. I think he has become somewhat wise. He told me that knowledge does not make a person wise….and that it is what you do with knowledge that does make one wise. That is approaching the edge of it. He is good for the world. Books are important. He now has experience to balance it all."

"And you? Where are you?" he asked of me.

"The Sea Change has set me over to being a Christian yogi, and becoming a better writer. And, of course, a secret weapon for you."

"Captain, you could have set up with one of those slinky women of Monte Carlo. Did you, perhaps, miss the boat? You did do a sojourn there."

"The rich will do anything, except share their wealth with you. After all, that is what makes them who they are. And they speak to hear what they have to say. Yacht or no yacht, the life of a pet dog is not for me. Besides, a yacht is not a fit ship for a sea Captain. The rich person runs the ship, and you; and the crew are just flunkies. What a sad lash-up! I could not abide it. Yet those long white sleekies in the Grebe shipyard are things of beauty in the eye of a sea Captain."

"And so you prefer poor widows?"

"Some of them are not so poor. But I never take their money. They need it to live on. I always hoped them to be happy and did have them become so too. Any lonely woman is my target for happiness. There are so many of them in the world…like grapes dying on the vine. I like to spark up their lives and make them alive. The sad thing is they want me to stay forever. The sea always calls me. It is the big beautiful woman."

"But a living woman has charms, physical ones too. You seem to know how to handle them too."

"Yes, I do!" he said with a twinkle in his eye.

"Back in Corsica. You had Royalty and a stone house. Were there no suitable women there for you?"

"The island had little to give. What we could get to live on came from the sea. It surrounded us. We were in its lap. It was like our mother. Yet it had utter charm. So vast and mysterious! The sea became my love. It was so beautiful! It became my passion to get a ship! The island was not my place to be. I was born to be a sea captain! Voyaging out, I found a woman just like the sea—Lenora! But then the sea took her for its own. They are the same to me now."

"Captain, you are a romantic!"

"No, a sea Captain." He insisted. "Who loves lonely women."

"Where are we now with Costa Rica?"

"We have done all we can here." Lamont said. "Costa Rica is now moving down the road to modernization due to greed—which in time will prove to be more bumpy than the pot-hole roads they deplore here. The bright note is that they are holding on to Democracy. It's like the story about Sherlock Holmes and Watson. They are camping in England. The tent is put up and they go to sleep. After a few hours Holmes wakes Watson. He says to him, Look up to the sky and tell me what you see.' Watson looks and says 'I see millions of stars.' 'And what does that tell you?' 'It tells me the universe is vast, it is near 2 A.M., and we will have a nice day tomorrow. What does it tell you?' Homes says, 'You have overlooked the obvious. Someone has stolen our tent.' The government of Costa Rica looks up and sees millions of dollars from tourists and Tech development and product manufacturings. They fail to see that something and someone is stealing their country."

"We could kidnap the ship from the C.I.A. and sail the world." I said. "This would give us a lot more adventure. We could go see Tiee out in the Pacific islands. But they are all over. They would only take it back in some port. Let's try to get Dirk to go with us. He would know how to keep the ship in your hands."

"He does not have the mentality to take that long a vacation." The Captain informed me.

The Captain went to the University to see Ted. Willy and I went out to the ship for some time away from the city. Its location still retained remoteness. We missed Sporty. Our ship watcher, Juan's son, was happy to get away from the ship for awhile.

A few days later here comes Juan's son with the small boat. The Captain was in it, and a shocking surprise to us—we looked down into the sweet face of a famous movie actress. She came aboard with

Lamont. He carried some lovely flowers and champagne. She had come down from Las Vegas previously, only to miss the ship at Wilmington Harbor.

"We have the fairest light from the Aurora Borealis that is Las Vegas visiting us." The Captain said. "We met there when the ship was anchored in Wilmington Harbor, and I took a trip up to Vegas for a look see. She was the most fair flower blooming in that garden of lights."

"Climbing up that rope ladder is like going up Mt. Rainier." She said to Willy and me. "That is some mountain! So massively beautiful and ever snowy....an ice-clad volcano!"

"Have been up there a number of times." I told her. "I love its beauty and dangers."

She walked around the ship, looking at everything. It excited her. She knew about it being a movie ship for "Harpoon." She knew about the Horn incident. She was in awe of our Captain. She had to come and see the ship.

"Do not locate near Mt. Rainer." The Captain warned her. "It's going to blow soon, and the Lahore will be tremendous. A hundred miles is too close. Puget Sound will see its effects. There is a lake inside that mountain. Steam vents are going near the top. It is getting more active right along."

The Captain had Willy put a mattress up in the bow, plus some drinks and sandwiches. They settled down to some long talking. They were telling each other a load of things...like two peas in a pod up there.

Willy and I kept back from the bow. It was the natural thing to do. I knew what the Captain was doing. He was at the top of the woman mountain seeking the Lost Lenora. There was no higher place to go now. Many men dreamed of where he was. She was lovely, sweet, intelligent, and famous to all in the entire world. She had made a lot of exciting movies for all the dreamers. To even meet her somewhere in society would make some men faint away.

From a good distance I was able to see her million dollar legs waving in the air. I was hoping. Willy was not seeing it too. The Seventh Heaven was happening. She would never be the same again. She was with the lover of the Ages. She most likely did not know his heart was buried in the sea.

She kissed Willy and me.

"Promise not to tell on me?" She was a sweet and decent person.

We agreed.

Just before daybreak, sneak agents boarded the "Flying Kate" and threw Juan's son overboard. They ran the ship down the Nicoya Gulf and out to the deep sea. There they blew the ship up. It sank in deep waters. The "Flying Kate" would fly across the sea no more. They left the area in their small boat, going up the coast toward Nicaragua. Now the Captain had lost his second love. Only the sea was left.

I thought of Ted's small, but wonderful, library aboard. It had been our pride. Ted would be so angry he would take Steve's place now. At least the Captain's beautiful Bible was not lost. He had it with him.

There were tears in the Captain's eyes. His Command Confidence seemed remote. He gave me his Bible.

"Here, take this Bible." He said. "And use it often. I no longer need it. It is in my heart with Lenora."

What was happening? He had never mentioned her name before. I was thinking that the loss of the ship had really upset him.

"I want you to meet me on the beach at Manuel Antonio park tonight." He told me.

It was a beautiful night. The full moon was up over the sea.

He came dressed up, with his black Homberg hat on. He smiled, and put his hand on my shoulder.

"My dear friend, I am going to write something down for you. Forgive me for stealing it out of your poetry."

He wrote for a brief time on a pad. I knew then what was happening, but would not, could not stop it.

The sparkle of starlight strikes the sea surface
It turns to shimmer
The Heavens Come Down to Earth
Bright is the night with God's light
How sweet the light sparkling up the night
Perfect light amid the darkening earth
GOD YOU ARE HERE!

The Captain walked across the beach and into the calm sea. I heard him saying "Lenora, Lenora, I see your sweet face in the shining waters of the sea…." He kept walking until only the black hat was floating on the bright surface of the sea.

> "But O, the ship,
> the immortal ship!
>
> O ship aboard
> The ship!
>
> Ship of the body,
> Ship of the soul,
>
> Voyaging, voyaging,
> Voyaging."
>
> --Walt Whitman

EPILOUGE

A WRITER PUTS FLESH ON THE BARE BONES OF A STORY

IS THE STORY THEN LESS TRUE, OR MORE TRUE?

(Willy became the Fire Chief in Oak Lawn. Ted the principal of the High School. Not true names. Only true names in book are: Bohne, Lamont, Capone. Wilmington Harbor is gone with the wind. It has become a dangerous Hispanic ghetto.)

ABOUT THE AUTHOR

The author is a Guadalcanal Marine (Fleet Marine Force), a newspaper reporter, editor, news photographer. He was a top Journalism student at Northwestern University in Evanston, Illinois. Prior to becoming a novelist, he wrote and published near 100 poems in various publications and in several categories. (16 are available at www.poetry.com) Poems are unusual ones. He studied Hemingway, William Blake, Somerset Maugham, and Shakespeare. Over many years he lived in every part of the vast U.S.A. and Canada, and went on dangerous adventures over half the world. He has a 4000 page First Edition Journal...which will go to 20,000 pages in time. It is a record of life experiences, wisdom sayings, amazing concepts, and various Remembrances. In "The Sea Change" he even presents a plan to restructure the societies of the world, but keeps the action of the story moving fast and powerful! He is planning 4 more novels and a series of amazing original short stories, plus "Tales of Guadalcanal."

9 780759 602359